Poet to Poet
Crabbe Selected by C. Day L

GEORGE CRABBE (1754–1832) began his literary career
in London in 1780, and took orders in 1781. From 1782
he lived outside London, first as chaplain to the Duke of
Rutland at Belvoir and later as Vicar of Trowbridge in
Wiltshire. One of his best known poems, *The Village*,
was published in 1783, but his reputation was really
established in 1807 with the publication of his *Poems*.
'Peter Grimes', one of his most popular works, is one
section from a twenty-four part poem, *The Borough*.

CECIL DAY LEWIS, poet, critic, novelist and translator,
was born in Ireland in 1904 and died in 1972. Educated
at Sherborne and Wadham College, Oxford, he was one of
the group of poets which included Auden and Spender.
His first volume, published in 1925, was followed by a
substantial number of volumes of poetry, critical works
and novels. His best known collections of poems are *From
Feathers to Iron* (1931), *Word Over All* (1943), *The Room
and Other Poems* (1965) and *The Whispering Roots* (1970).
Under the pseudonym, Nicholas Blake, he also wrote
a number of murder mysteries. He was appointed Poet
Laureate in 1968. A selection of his poems is published
in Penguins.

CRABBE

Selected by
C. Day Lewis

Penguin Books

Penguin Books Ltd, Harmondsworth,
Middlesex, England
Penguin Books Inc., 7110 Ambassador Road,
Baltimore, Maryland 21207, U.S.A.
Penguin Books Australia Ltd, Ringwood,
Victoria, Australia

First published 1973
Selection copyright © Penguin Books Ltd, 1973
Introduction copyright © the Estate of C. Day Lewis, 1973

Made and printed in Great Britain by
Cox & Wyman Ltd, London, Reading and Fakenham
Set in Monotype Ehrhardt

Contents

Introduction

George Crabbe was born in Aldeburgh, Suffolk, on Christmas Eve, 1754. His father was a collector of salt-duties and also owned a warehouse in which the poet worked for short periods in his youth. Though Crabbe was a bookish child, his father apprenticed him at the age of fourteen to a surgeon, who used his apprentices chiefly for work on his farm near Bury St Edmunds. When he was eighteen Crabbe met Sarah Elmy, whom he was to marry in 1783. His first visit to London, when he walked the hospitals and picked up such surgical knowledge as he could, ended in less than a year. Back he came to Aldeburgh, which was the source of so much of his poetry and where his life-long interest in botany began, to practise a profession for which he had neither skill nor inclination.

In 1779 he decided to give up this unrewarding profession and try his luck as a writer. So he set off for London again, with a few poems he had written, a box of clothes, a case of surgical instruments and three pounds he had borrowed from a Mr Dudley North. Crabbe, a provincial young man, proud, awkward, unsophisticated, with none of the advantages of rank or education to aid him, could hardly be expected to make an impression on literary circles. For a year he lived in extreme poverty, receiving little encouragement and less recognition. His poems were rejected by publishers, and when at last 'The Candidate' appeared in print, reviewers thought little of it and its publisher failed. Crabbe was reduced to applying for patronage to Lord North, then to Lord Shelburne, then to

Lord Chancellor Thurlow. Unavailingly. It was at this nadir of his fortunes that Crabbe write *The Poet's Journal*, which his son printed posthumously in his father's *Life*. 'It's the vilest thing in the world,' wrote the poet, 'to have but one coat.'

From these desperate circumstances he was rescued by Edmund Burke, to whom he had written as a last desperate throw. The great statesman 'immediately appointed an hour ... to call upon him at his house in London; and the short interview that ensued, entirely, and for ever, changed the nature of his wordly fortunes'. Burke received the young poet into his house, introduced him to other persons of influence, criticized his work with discrimination, advised and helped him to take holy orders, and put him in the way of ecclesiastical preferment. In 1783 Crabbe was able to marry his Sarah. The lean years were over.

From a curacy at Aldeburgh Crabbe went on to become domestic chaplain to the Duke of Rutland. It was while he lived at Belvoir Castle that Crabbe published *The Village*, his first runaway success and in many ways his finest poem, over which Dr Johnson had given him some magisterial advice. Shortly after this, Lord Thurlow presented him with two small livings in Dorset. (Crabbe, like most clergymen of his day, saw nothing wrong in pluralism.) When he married, he and Sarah did not reside long at Belvoir. As his son remarked, 'neither nature nor circumstances had qualified' his father for the office of private chaplain. 'The aristocracy of genius approaches too near the aristocracy of station.' He therefore took the curacy of Stathern and presently moved from there to his rectory at Muston, ministering not only to the spiritual needs of the parishioners but also employing his medical knowledge to attend them in sickness. At this period, after the publication of *The Newspaper*, Crabbe 'buried himself completely in the obscurity of domestic and village life', publishing nothing for twenty-two years: although a number of manuscripts were completed, including what would have been an authoritative book on botany, all were consigned to the flames.

To what extent this long silence was due to his wife's failing health, we cannot be sure. After her death in 1813, Crabbe moved away from Suffolk altogether and spent the rest of his life as rector of Trowbridge, re-entering the literary world in London, fêted by Tom Moore, Rogers, Scott and other celebrities, botanizing and fossilizing, voluminously writing, conscientiously performing his pastoral duties, happy with his sons and his grandchildren, till in 1832 he died.

As to the character of Crabbe and his work, two voices may be quoted. E. M. Forster wrote, 'He disapproved, he reproved ... Disapproval is all too common in the pulpit, but it is rare in poetry, and its presence gave Crabbe's work a curious flavour, subtle yet tart, which will always attract the connoisseur.' This aptitude for disapproval may be illustrated by Crabbe's first essay in verse, cautioning a young schoolfellow 'against being too much elevated about a new set of blue ribands to his straw bonnet'. Another way of seeing it is that 'Crabbe had an unusually active and acute moral sensibility ... He constantly judged what he saw, but feeling accompanied judgement, and he was accustomed to consider the susceptibilities even of those whose behaviour he condemned.' These views, expressed by Miss Lilian Heddakin in *The Poetry of Crabbe*, seem to me just.

Although Crabbe was called, in *Rejected Addresses*, 'Pope in worsted stockings', he had neither the temperament nor the pungency of style which are needed for satire. His aunt by marriage, Mrs Tovell, a formidable old battle-axe, boasted that she could 'screw Crabbe up and down like a fiddle': but his picture of her as 'the widow Goe' in *The Parish Register* has more of high-spirited fun than of real malice. In later life, writing to one of those ladies whom he used to address with a kind of stately flirtatiousness, he said of the characters in his poems, 'there is not one of whom I had not in my mind the original; but I was obliged, in some cases, to take them from their real situations, in one or two instances to change even their sex, and in many, the circumstances' – an expedient normal to most novelists, incidentally.

It was Crabbe's story-telling power which, together with his keen moral sensibility, so endeared his work to Jane Austen. In a letter to her sister Cassandra she wrote (21 October 1813), 'No, I have never seen the death of Mrs Crabbe. I have only just been making out from one of the prefaces that he was probably married. It is almost ridiculous. Poor woman! I will comfort *him* as well as I can, but I do not undertake to be good to her children. She had better not leave any.'*

Thomas Campbell noticed in Crabbe 'a vigilant shrewdness that almost eluded you by keeping its watch so quietly'; and this impression of a chief among us taking notes is borne out by Crabbe's proven powers of concentration, by his shyness in conversation (except when he was sure of the good will of the company), by his distaste for argument and controversy. This quiet attentiveness to individuals emerged through his verse tales, as a preoccupation with types. 'Character in action,' says Miss Heddakin, 'for Crabbe is not significant unless it manifests a passion or a moral quality.'

Pope was his model. But, apart from an occasional line such as 'Sick without pity, sorrowing without hope' or 'Laughing in languor, miserably gay', Crabbe is remarkably underivative. Just as he is sardonic where Pope is satirical, his tone one of asperity, rather than of wit, so his rhythms lack the variety and elasticity of Pope. The heroic couplets go treadling and tacking like a sewing-machine, with little change of tempo: the reader must stay wide awake to feel, through this rather hypnotic medium, the intensities and relaxations of each poem. It is not unlike the East Anglian countryside, where we have to look for the subtle variations of an apparently monotonous surface.

The force of many of Crabbe's story-poems is at least partly

* *Letters*, ed. R. W. Chapman, Oxford, 1932, 2. 358.

derived from this blend of melodramatic or 'sensational' plot with a quiet decorum of diction. Crabbe, though generally cool towards the Lake poets, did come to admire Wordsworth greatly: but, having seldom very far to fall, his work does not suffer from the stunning bathos to which Wordsworth occasionally fell victim. It is here, too, that Crabbe's decorum saves him from the abysses into which the Romantic poets could tumble. He has been called a miniaturist, and his poems compared with the paintings of Dutch interiors. The latter is the more accurate judgement. His work has the sombre glow, the calm, the precision of realistic detail which we find in the Dutch masters; and it is the down-to-earth realism of their subject matter which most of all gives Crabbe's best poems their distinctive quality.

Crabbe's originality was certainly not of diction. Dwelling as it were on a watershed between classical and romantic poetry, his streams all flowed the old way. His originality – and it is a very remarkable one – is in his subject. Low life had been almost invariably treated in poetry for its comic values: Crabbe was the first poet to be absorbed exclusively (till *The Tales of the Hall*) in the life of the poor, the destitute, or the 'common man'. Novel, highly unorthodox subjects, treated in an exceptionally sober and conservative idiom – this was surely what gave *The Village* its resounding success. Crabbe's early poem – a counterblast to Goldsmith's *Deserted Village* – gains added strength in its picture of the rural poor, because he excluded from it any overt expression of his own feelings. Book I of this poem is all the more effective because the indignation and pity behind it are all channelled into the verse itself, fertilizing and heightening it.

Yet, for all the revolutionary context of his poems, Crabbe was very much the conventional man of his period – a Whig, it is true, but a traditionalist, a Church of England parson even more suspicious of religious enthusiasm than of Deism (though he came to be tolerant towards individual Dissenters), a poet who put reason before emotion – the kind of poet exemplified in the passage with which this selection opens. In developing this proper study of mankind through his verse, he sought for a realism which should engage the reader's sympathetic interest but should not strike home so hard as 'to create painful sensations' in him. Crabbe allows there is a higher kind of poetry, which depends upon inspiration: but this does not invalidate his own productions – the kind of poetry that appeals to the reader's good sense rather than to his imagination.

After his twenty-two-year silence, though he never quite resumed the indignation or equalled the vivid colours of the best lines in *The Village*, Crabbe broadened his purview, greatly extending and diversifying the range of characters he wrote about. Both *The Parish Register* and *The Borough* contain many passages which can strike us as forcibly as they struck Crabbe's contemporaries. We can see his scepticism about the medical profession, the cold, analytic eye he casts upon greed, hypocrisy and meanness, his hatred of cruelty. *Peter Grimes* has an immediacy about it, a sense of personal involvement never found in any other of those story-poems, which makes me feel that Crabbe encountered just such a man during his days at Aldeburgh. Some of the *Tales*, with which he followed *The Borough*, display strong intuition or psychological knowledge; even when their plots are feuilleton-ish and unreal few of them lack passages which probe well below the surface of human nature. The subsequent volumes – *Tales of the Hall* and the posthumous *Tales* – show a greater verisimilitude sometimes than their predecessors but have, for me, less hitting power, less bite.

In making a selection from the voluminous work of this poet, the editor is faced with several problems. Most of the poems being narratives running to a considerable length, one could not accommodate many of them complete in a volume of the required size. Would the selection be more representative of

Crabbe by choosing a few of the narratives and reproducing
them at full length, or by picking short passages from a greater
number of them? I decided on the latter, including in full only
Book I of *The Village*, *The Parish Clerk*, *Peter Grimes*, and *Delay
Has Danger*. This should give the reader a sufficient idea of the
strategy Crabbe employed over the extent of a whole poem;
for the rest, I chose passages which seemed to me specially
lively from a considerable number of stories, hoping they may
persuade the reader to look up the poems of which they are part.

'Sir Eustace Grey', a sustained effort of the imagination
equalled only by Cowper's 'The Castaway', is a poem quite
outside Crabbe's normal range. Unlike Cowper's poem, 'Sir
Eustace Grey' has nothing subjective about it. From this
study of a mind crazed by guilt I have taken a number of
stanzas which portray the madman's hallucinations: they read
like some drug-born experiences. Crabbe himself started tak-
ing opiates for digestive trouble early in his married life: 'to
a constant but slightly increasing dose,' his son wrote, 'may be
attributed his long and generally healthy life.' These stanzas
show how expertly Crabbe could use a ballad-type metre, and
make one regret that he did not use it more often.

Another problem has to do with the monotony of the med-
ium, the bulk of Crabbe's verse being written in heroic coup-
lets. To younger readers in particular, more accustomed to the
irregular metres or free verse of their contemporaries, this is
likely to be an obstacle to the full enjoyment of Crabbe. But it is
not insuperable. It looks as if the craft of versification – as
opposed to the art of poetry – is in England and America dying
of neglect. Yet, if the modern ear is deaf to the subtlety at work
within Crabbe's apparently monotonous style, one's mind can
respond to the humour, the fine shades of meaning, the delicate
moral and psychological discriminations, and no less the forth-
right plain speaking, which abound in his poems.

Apart from the passage about the Poet, taken from *The
Borough*, which I put at the start of this selection, and the

fragment called 'Infancy', with which I end it, the poems and extracts are printed in chronological order of the publication of the volumes in which they originally appeared. The first of these passages can be taken as summing up Crabbe's ideas on his own vocation, which he sees very much as Pope's 'The proper study of mankind is man'. 'Infancy' is almost certainly auto-biographical, leading up to an episode of the poet's own childhood:

> I see the griefs that seize their subject Man,
> That in the weeping Child their early reign began.

Immediately before 'Infancy' I have placed a simple and touching lyric, 'Parham Revisited', which recalls the greatest grief of Crabbe's life, the death of his beloved wife.

Crabbe's scientific studies, as well as the bent of the times in which he grew up, inclined him to believe in the paramount place of reason in human affairs. This may seem today an eccentric position for a poet to take up. What about feeling, what about the passions? Well, there it is: Crabbe thought the poet's business was not to give way to or exploit 'the Proteus-passions', but, studying them objectively, to show 'what strange waste of life and joy they make'. He by no means considered that the poet must himself experience all 'these turns and movements of the human heart' which provide the subjects for his *Tales*. As his poetry displays a balance and decorum in its versification, so his moral ideal is a kind of normality to which every civilized being should aspire. This, when one looks at the desperate expedients and experiments of poets (and others) today, is at least refreshing.

C. DAY LEWIS

The Borough (1810)

from Schools

For this the poet looks the world around,
Where form and life and reasoning man are found:
He loves the mind, in all its modes, to trace,
And all the manners of the changing race;
Silent he walks the road of life along,
And views the aims of its tumultuous throng:
He finds what shapes the Proteus-passions take,
And what strange waste of life and joy they make,
And loves to show them in their varied ways,
With honest blame or with unflattering praise.
'Tis good to know, 'tis pleasant to impart,
These turns and movements of the human heart:
The stronger features of the soul to paint,
And make distinct the latent and the faint;
Man as he is, to place in all men's view,
Yet none with rancour, none with scorn pursue:
Nor be it ever of my portraits told –
'Here the strong lines of malice we behold.'

from The Choice

What vulgar title thus salutes the eye,
The schoolboy's first attempt at poesy?
The long-worn theme of every humbler Muse,
For wits to scorn and nurses to peruse;
The dull description of a scribbler's brain,
And sigh'd-for-wealth, for which he sighs in vain;
A glowing chart of fairy-land estate,
Romantic scenes, and visions out of date,
Clear skies, clear streams, soft banks, and sober bowers,
Deer, whimpering brooks, and wind-perfuming flowers?

Not thus! too long have I in fancy wove
My slender webs of wealth, and peace, and love;
Have dream'd of plenty, in the midst of want,
And sought, by Hope, what Hope can never grant,
Been fool'd by wishes, and still wish'd again,
And loved the flattery, while I knew it vain!
'Gain by the Muse!' – alas! thou might'st as soon
Pluck gain (as Percy honour) from the moon;
As soon grow rich by ministerial nods,
As soon divine by dreaming of the gods,
As soon succeed by telling ladies truth,
Or preaching moral documents to youth:
To as much purpose, mortal! thy desires,
As Tully's flourishes to country squires;
As simple truth within St James's state,
Or the soft lute in shrill-tongued Billingsgate.
'Gain by the Muse!' alas, preposterous hope!
Who ever gain'd by poetry – but Pope?

from The Library

Say ye, who search these records of the dead,
Who read huge works, to boast what ye have read;
Can all the real knowledge ye possess,
Or those (if such there are) who more than guess,
Atone for each impostor's wild mistakes,
And mend the blunders pride or folly makes?
What thought so wild, what airy dream so light,
That will not prompt a theorist to write?
What art so prevalent, what proof so strong,
That will convince him his attempt is wrong?
One in the solids finds each lurking ill,
Nor grants the passive fluids power to kill;
A learned friend some subtler reason brings,
Absolves the channels, but condemns their springs;
The subtle nerves, that shun the doctor's eye,
Escape no more his subtler theory;
The vital heat, that warms the labouring heart,
Lends a fair system to these sons of art;
The vital air, a pure and subtile stream,
Serves a foundation for an airy scheme,
Assists the doctor, and supports his dream.
Some have their favourite ills, and each disease
Is but a younger branch that kills from these:
One to the gout contracts all human pain,
He views it raging in the frantic brain;
Finds it in fevers all his efforts mar,
And sees it lurking in the cold catarrh:
Bilious by some, by others nervous seen,
Rage the fantastic demons of the spleen;

And every symptom of the strange disease
With every system of the sage agrees.
   Ye frigid tribe, on whom I wasted long
The tedious hours and ne'er indulged in song;
Ye first seducers of my easy heart,
Who promised knowledge ye could not impart;
Ye dull deluders, truth's destructive foes;
Ye sons of fiction, clad in stupid prose;
Ye treacherous leaders, who, yourselves in doubt,
Light up false fires, and send us far about; –
Still may yon spider round your pages spin,
Subtile and slow, her emblematic gin!
Buried in dust and lost in silence, dwell,
Most potent, grave, and reverend friends – farewell!

The Village

The Village Life, and every care that reigns
O'er youthful peasants and declining swains;
What labour yields, and what, that labour past,
Age, in its hour of languor, finds at last;
What form the real picture of the poor,
Demand a song – the Muse can give no more.

Fled are those times, when, in harmonious strains,
The rustic poet praised his native plains:
No shepherds now, in smooth alternate verse,
Their country's beauty or their nymphs' rehearse;
Yet still for these we frame the tender strain,
Still in our lays fond Corydons complain,
And shepherds' boys their amorous pains reveal
The only pains, alas! they never feel.

On Mincio's banks, in Caesar's bounteous reign,
If Tityrus found the Golden Age again,
Must sleepy bards the flattering dream prolong,
Mechanic echoes of the Mantuan song?
From Truth and Nature shall we widely stray,
Where Virgil, not where Fancy, leads the way?

Yes, thus the Muses sing of happy swains,
Because the Muses never knew their pains:
They boast their peasants' pipes; but peasants now
Resign their pipes and plod behind the plough;
And few, amid the rural-tribe, have time
To number syllables, and play with rhyme;
Save honest Duck, what son of verse could share
The poet's rapture, and the peasant's care?
Or the great labours of the field degrade,
With the new peril of a poorer trade?

From this chief cause these idle praises spring,

That themes so easy few forbear to sing;
For no deep thought the trifling subjects ask;
To sing of shepherds is an easy task:
The happy youth assumes the common strain,
A nymph his mistress, and himself a swain;
With no sad scenes he clouds his tuneful prayer,
But all, to look like her, is painted fair.

I grant indeed that fields and flocks have charms
For him that grazes or for him that farms;
But when amid such pleasing scenes I trace
The poor laborious natives of the place,
And see the mid-day sun, with fervid ray,
On their bare heads and dewy temples play;
While some, with feebler heads and fainter hearts,
Deplore their fortune, yet sustain their parts:
Then shall I dare these real ills to hide
In tinsel trappings of poetic pride?

No; cast by Fortune on a frowning coast,
Which neither groves nor happy valleys boast;
Where other cares than those the Muse relates,
And other shepherds dwell with other mates;
By such examples taught, I paint the Cot,
As Truth will paint it, and as Bards will not:
Nor you, ye poor, of letter'd scorn complain,
To you the smoothest song is smooth in vain;
O'ercome by labour, and bow'd down by time,
Feel you the barren flattery of a rhyme?
Can poets soothe you, when you pine for bread,
By winding myrtles round your ruin'd shed?
Can their light tales your weighty griefs o'erpower,
Or glad with airy mirth with the toilsome hour?

Lo! where the heath, with withering brake grown o'er,
Lends the light turf that warms the neighbouring poor;
From thence a length of burning sand appears,
Where the thin harvest waves its wither'd ears;

Rank weeds, that every art and care defy,
Reign o'er the land, and rob the blighted rye:
There thistles stretch their prickly arms afar,
And to the ragged infant threaten war;
There poppies nodding, mock the hope of toil;
There the blue bugloss paints the sterile soil;
Hardy and high, above the slender sheaf,
The slimy mallow waves her silky leaf;
O'er the young shoot the charlock throws a shade,
And clasping tares cling round the sickly blade;
With mingled tints the rocky coasts abound,
And a sad splendour vainly shines around.
So looks the nymph whom wretched arts adorn,
Betray'd by man, then left for man to scorn;
Whose cheek in vain assumes the mimic rose,
While her sad eyes the troubled breast disclose;
Whose outward splendour is but folly's dress,
Exposing most, when most it gilds distress.

Here joyless roam a wild amphibious race,
With sullen wo display'd in every face;
Who, far from civil arts and social fly,
And scowl at strangers with suspicious eye.

Here too the lawless merchant of the main
Draws from his plough th' intoxicated swain;
Want only claim'd the labour of the day,
But vice now steals his nightly rest away.

Where are the swains, who, daily labour done,
With rural games play'd down the setting sun;
Who struck with matchless force the bounding ball,
Or made the pond'rous quoit obliquely fall;
While some huge Ajax, terrible and strong,
Engaged some artful stripling of the throng,
And fell beneath him, foil'd, while far around
Hoarse triumph rose, and rocks return'd the sound?
Where now are these? – Beneath yon cliff they stand,

To show the freighted pinnace where to land;
To load the ready steed with guilty haste,
To fly in terror o'er the pathless waste,
Or, when detected, in their straggling course,
To foil their foes by cunning or by force;
Or, yielding part (which equal knaves demand),
To gain a lawless passport through the land.

Here, wand'ring long, amid these frowning fields,
I sought the simple life that Nature yields;
Rapine and Wrong and Fear usurp'd her place,
And a bold, artful, surly, savage race;
Who, only skill'd to take the finny tribe,
The yearly dinner, or septennial bribe,
Wait on the shore, and, as the waves run high,
On the tost vessel bend their eager eye,
Which to their coast directs its venfrous way;
Theirs, or the ocean's, miserable prey.

As on their neighbouring beach yon swallows stand,
And wait for favouring winds to leave the land;
While still for flight the ready wing is spread:
So waited I the favouring hour, and fled;
Fled from these shores where guilt and famine reign,
And cried, Ah! hapless they who still remain;
Who still remain to hear the ocean roar,
Whose greedy waves devour the lessening shore;
Till some fierce tide, with more imperious sway,
Sweeps the low hut and all it holds away;
When the sad tenant weeps from door to door,
And begs a poor protection from the poor!

But these are scenes where Nature's niggard hand
Gave a spare portion to the famish'd land;
Hers is the fault, if here mankind complain
Of fruitless toil and labour spent in vain;
But yet in other scenes more fair in view,
Where Plenty smiles – alas! she smiles for few –

And those who taste not, yet behold her store,
Are as the slaves that dig the golden ore, –
The wealth around them makes them doubly poor.

  Or will you deem them amply paid in health,
Labour's fair child, that languishes with wealth?
Go then! and see them rising with the sun,
Through a long course of daily toil to run;
See them beneath the dog-star's raging heat,
When the knees tremble and the temples beat;
Behold them, leaning on their scythes, look o'er
The labour past, and toils to come explore;
See them alternate suns and showers engage,
And hoard up aches and anguish for their age;
Through fens and marshy moors their steps pursue,
When their warm pores imbibe the evening dew;
Then own that labour may as fatal be
To these thy slaves, as thine excess to thee.

  Amid this tribe too oft a manly pride
Strives in strong toil the fainting heart to hide;
There may you see the youth of slender frame
Contend with weakness, weariness, and shame;
Yet, urged along, and proudly loth to yield,
He strives to join his fellows of the field.
Till long-contending nature droops at last,
Declining health rejects his poor repast,
His cheerless spouse the coming danger sees,
And mutual murmurs urge the slow disease.

  Yet grant them health, 'tis not for us to tell,
Though the head droops not, that the heart is well;
Or will you praise that homely, healthy fare,
Plenteous and plain, that happy peasants share!
Oh! trifle not with wants you cannot feel,
Nor mock the misery of a stinted meal;
Homely, not wholesome, plain, not plenteous, such
As you who praise would never deign to touch.

Ye gentle souls, who dream of rural ease,
Whom the smooth stream and smoother sonnet please;
Go! if the peaceful cot your praises share,
Go look within, and ask if peace be there;
If peace be his – that drooping weary sire,
Or theirs, that offspring round their feeble fire;
Or hers, that matron pale, whose trembling hand
Turns on the wretched hearth th' expiring brand!
Nor yet can Time itself obtain for these
Life's latest comforts, due respect and ease;
For yonder see that hoary swain, whose age
Can with no cares except his own engage;
Who, propp'd on that rude staff, looks up to see
The bare arms broken from the withering tree,
On which, a boy, he climb'd the loftiest bough,
Then his first joy, but his sad emblem now,
He once was chief in all the rustic trade;
His steady hand the straightest furrow made;
Full many a prize he won, and still is proud
To find the triumphs of his youth allow'd;
A transient pleasure sparkles in his eyes,
He hears and smiles, then thinks again and sighs:
For now he journeys to his grave in pain;
The rich disdain him; nay, the poor disdain:
Alternate masters now their slave command,
Urge the weak efforts of his feeble hand,
And, when his age attempts its task in vain,
With ruthless taunts, of lazy poor complain.
Oft may you see him, when he tends the sheep,
His winter-charge, beneath the hillock weep;
Oft hear him murmur to the winds that blow
O'er his white locks and bury them in snow,
When, roused by rage and muttering in the morn,
He mends the broken hedge with icy thorn: –
    'Why do I live, when I desire to be

At once from life and life's long labour free?
Like leaves in spring, the young are blown away,
Without the sorrows of a slow decay;
I, like yon wither'd leaf, remain behind,
Nipp'd by the frost, and shivering in the wind;
There it abides till younger buds come on,
As I, now all my fellow-swains are gone;
Then, from the rising generation thrust,
It falls, like me, unnoticed to the dust.
     'These fruitful fields, these numerous flocks I see,
Are others' gain, but killing cares to me;
To me the children of my youth are lords,
Cool in their looks, but hasty in their words:
Wants of their own demand their care; and who
Feels his own want and succours others too?
A lonely, wretched man, in pain I go,
None need my help, and none relieve my wo;
Then let my bones beneath the turf be laid,
And men forget the wretch they would not aid.'
     Thus groan the old, till, by disease oppress'd,
They taste a final wo, and then they rest.
     Theirs is yon house that holds the parish-poor,
Whose walls of mud scarce bear the broken door;
There, where the putrid vapours, flagging, play,
And the dull wheel hums doleful through the day; —
There children dwell who know no parents' care;
Parents, who know no children's love, dwell there!
Heartbroken matrons on their joyless bed,
Forsaken wives, and mothers never wed;
Dejected widows with unheeded tears,
And crippled age with more than childhood fears;
The lame, the blind, and, far the happiest they!
The moping idiot and the madman gay.
Here too sick their final doom receive,
Here brought, amid the scenes of grief, to grieve,

Where the loud groans from some sad chamber flow,
Mix'd with the clamours of the crowd below;
Here, sorrowing, they each kindred sorrow scan,
And the cold charities of man to man:
Whose laws indeed for ruin'd age provide,
And strong compulsion plucks the scrap from pride;
But still that scrap is bought with many a sigh,
And pride embitters what it can't deny.

 Say ye, oppress'd by some fantastic woes,
Some jarring nerve that baffles your repose;
Who press the downy couch, while slaves advance
With timid eye, to read the distant glance;
Who with sad prayers the weary doctor tease,
To name the nameless ever-new disease;
Who with mock patience dire complaints endure,
Which real pain and that alone can cure;
How would ye bear in real pain to lie,
Despised, neglected, left alone to die?
How would ye bear to draw your latest breath,
Where all that's wretched paves the way for death?

 Such is that room which one rude beam divides,
And naked rafters form the sloping sides;
Where the vile bands that blind the thatch are seen,
And lath and mud are all that lie between;
Save one dull pane, that, coarsely patch'd, gives way
To the rude tempest, yet excludes the day:
Here, on a matted flock, with dust o'erspread,
The dropping wretch reclines his languid head;
For him no hand the cordial cup applies,
Or wipes the tear that stagnates in his eyes;
No friends with soft discourse his pain beguile,
Or promise hope till sickness wears a smile.

 But soon a loud and hasty summons calls,
Shakes the thin roof, and echoes round the walls;
Anon, a figure enters, quaintly neat,

All pride and business, bustle and conceit;
With looks unalter'd by these scenes of wo,
With speed that, entering, speaks his haste to go,
He bids the gazing throng around him fly,
And carries fate and physic in his eye:
A potent quack, long versed in human ills,
Who first insults the victim whom he kills;
Whose murd'rous hand a drowsy Bench protect,
And whose most tender mercy is neglect.

Paid by the parish for attendance here,
He wears contempt upon his sapient sneer;
In haste he seeks the bed where Misery lies,
Impatience mark'd in his averted eyes;
And, some habitual queries hurried o'er,
Without reply, he rushes on the door:
His drooping patient, long inured to pain,
And long unheeded, knows remonstrance vain;
He ceases now the feeble help to crave
Of man; and silent sinks into the grave.

But ere his death some pious doubts arise,
Some simple fears, which 'bold bad' men despise;
Fain would he ask the parish-priest to prove
His title certain to the joys above:
For this he sends the murmuring nurse, who calls
The holy stranger to these dismal walls:
And doth not he, the pious man, appear,
He, 'passing rich with forty pounds a year?'
Ah! no; a shepherd of a different stock,
And far unlike him, feeds this little flock:
A jovial youth, who thinks his Sunday's task
As much as God or man can fairly ask;
The rest he gives to loves and labours light,
To fields the morning, and to feasts the night;
None better skill'd the noisy pack to guide,
To urge their chase, to cheer them or to chide;

A sportsman keen, he shoots through half the day,
And, skill'd at whist, devotes the night to play:
Then, while such honours bloom around his head,
Shall he sit sadly by the sick man's bed,
To raise the hope he feels not, or with zeal
To combat fears that e'en the pious feel?
   Now once again the gloomy scene explore,
Less gloomy now; the bitter hour is o'er,
The man of many sorrows sighs no more. –
Up yonder hill, behold how sadly slow
The bier moves winding from the vale below;
There lie the happy dead, from trouble free,
And the glad parish pays the frugal fee:
No more, O Death! thy victim starts to hear
Churchwarden stern, or kingly overseer;
No more the farmer claims his humble bow,
Thou art his lord, the best of tyrants thou!
   Now to the church behold the mourners come,
Sedately torpid and devoutly dumb;
The village children now their games suspend,
To see the bier that bears their ancient friend;
For he was one in all their idle sport,
And like a monarch ruled their little court,
The pliant bow he form'd, the flying ball,
The bat, the wicket, were his labours all;
Him now they follow to his grave, and stand
Silent and sad, and gazing, hand in hand;
While bending low, their eager eyes explore
The mingled relics of the parish poor:
The bell tolls late, the moping owl flies round,
Fear marks the flight and magnifies the sound;
The busy priest, detain'd by weightier care,
Defers his duty till the day of prayer;
And, waiting long, the crowd retire distress'd,
To think a poor man's bones should lie unbless'd.

from The Newspaper

So charm the News; but we, who, far from town,
Wait till the postman brings the packet down,
Once in the week, a vacant day behold,
And stay for tidings, till they're three days old:
That day arrives; no welcome post appears,
But the dull morn a sullen aspect wears;
We meet, but ah! without our wonted smile,
To talk of headaches, and complain of bile;
Sullen we ponder o'er a dull repast,
Nor feast the body while the mind must fast.
  A master-passion is the love of news,
Not music so commands, nor so the Muse:
Give poets claret, they grow idle soon;
Feed the musician, and he's out of tune;
But the sick mind, of this disease possess'd,
Flies from all cure, and sickens when at rest.
  Now sing, my Muse, what various parts compose
These rival sheets of politics and prose.
  First, from each brother's hoard a part they draw,
A mutual theft that never fear'd a law;
Whate'er they gain, to each man's portion fall,
And read it once, you read it through them all:
For this their runners ramble day and night,
To drag each lurking deed to open light;
For daily bread the dirty trade they ply,
Coin their fresh tales, and live upon the lie:
Like bees for honey, forth for news they spring, –
Industrious creatures! ever on the wing;
Home to their several cells they bear the store,

Cull'd of all kinds, then roam abroad for more.
   No anxious virgin flies to 'fair Tweedside;'
No injured husband mourns his faithless bride;
No duel dooms the fiery youth to bleed;
But through the town transpires each vent'rous deed.
   Should some fair frail-one drive her prancing pair,
Where rival peers contend to please the fair;
When, with new force, she aids her conquering eyes,
And beauty decks, with all that beauty buys;
Quickly we learn whose heart her influence feels,
Whose acres melt before her glowing wheels.
   To these a thousand idle themes succeed,
Deeds of all kinds, and comments to each deed,
Here stocks, the state-barometers, we view,
That rise or fall, by causes known to few;
Promotion's ladder who goes up or down;
Who wed, or who seduced, amuse the town;
What new-born heir has made his father blest;
What heir exults, his father now at rest;
That ample list the Tyburn-herald gives,
And each known knave, who still for Tyburn lives.
   So grows the work, and now the printer tries
His powers no more, but leans on his allies.
   When lo! the advertising tribe succeed,
Pay to be read, yet find but few will read;
And chief th' illustrious race, whose drops and pills
Have patent powers to vanquish human ills.
These, with their cures, a constant aid remain,
To bless the pale composer's fertile brain;
Fertile it is, but still the noblest soil
Requires some pause, some intervals from toil;
And they at least a certain ease obtain
From Katterfelto's skill, and Graham's glowing strain.
   I too must aid, and pay to see my name
Hung in these dirty avenues to fame;

Nor pay in vain, if aught the Muse has seen,
And sung, could make those avenues more clean;
Could stop one slander ere it found its way,
And gave to public scorn its helpless prey.
By the same aid, the Stage invites her friends,
And kindly tells the banquet she intends;
Thither from real life the many run,
With Siddons weep, or laugh with Abingdon;
Pleased in fictitious joy or grief, to see
The mimic passion with their own agree;
To steal a few enchanted hours away
From care, and drop the curtain on the day,
    But who can steal from self that wretched wight,
Whose darling work is tried, some fatal night?
Most wretchéd man! when, bane to every bliss,
He hears the serpent-critic's rising hiss;
Then groans succeed: not traitors on the wheel
Can feel like him, or have such pangs to feel.
Nor end they here: next day he reads his fall
In every paper; critics are they all;
He sees his branded name, with wild affright,
And hears again the cat-calls of the night.

The Parish Register

from Baptisms

To name an infant meet our village-sires,
Assembled all, as such event requires;
Frequent and full, the rural sages sate,
And speakers many urged the long debate, –
Some harden'd knaves, who roved the country round,
Had left a babe within the parish-bound. –
First, of the fact they question'd – 'Was it true?'
The child was brought – 'What then remain'd to do?
Was't dead or living?' This was fairly proved, –
'Twas pinch'd, it roar'd, and every doubt removed.
Then by what name th' unwelcome guest to call
Was long a question, and it posed them all;
For he who lent it to a babe unknown,
Censorious men might take it for his own:
They look'd about, they gravely spoke to all
And not one Richard answer'd to the call.
Next they inquired the day, when, passing by,
Th' unlucky peasant heard the stranger's cry;
This known, – how food and raiment they might give,
Was next debated – for the rogue would live;
At last, with all their words and work content,
Back to their homes the prudent vestry went,
And Richard Monday to the workhouse sent.
There was he pinch'd and pitied, thump'd and fed,
And duly took his beatings and his bread;
Patient in all control, in all abuse,
He found contempt and kicking have their use:
Sad, silent, supple; bending to the blow,
A slave of slaves, the lowest of the low;

His pliant soul gave way to all things base,
He knew no shame, he dreaded no disgrace.
It seem'd, so well his passions he suppress'd,
No feeling stirr'd his ever-torpid breast;
Him might the meanest pauper bruise and cheat,
He was a footstool for the beggar's feet;
His were the legs that ran at all commands;
They used on all occasion Richard's hands:
His very soul was not his own; he stole
As others order'd, and without a dole;
In all disputes, on either part he lied,
And freely pledged his oath on either side;
In all rebellions Richard join'd the rest,
In all detections Richard first confess'd:
Yet, though disgraced, he watch'd his time so well,
He rose in favour, when in fame he fell;
Base was his usage, vile his whole employ,
And all despised and fed the pliant boy.
At length, ''tis time he should abroad be sent,'
Was whisper'd near him, – and abroad he went;
One morn they call'd him, Richard answer'd not;
They deem'd him hanging, and in time forgot, –
Yet miss'd him long, as each, throughout the clan,
Found he 'had better spared a better man.'
   Now Richard's talents for the world were fit,
He'd no small cunning, and had some small wit;
Had that calm look which seem'd to all assent,
And that complacent speech which nothing meant:
He'd but one care, and that he strove to hide,
How best for Richard Monday to provide.
Steel, through opposing plates, the magnet draws,
And steely atoms culls from dust and straws;
And thus our hero, to his interest true,
Gold through all bars and from each trifle drew;
But still more surely round the world to go,

This fortune's child had neither friend nor foe.
　　Long lost to us, at last our man we trace, –
Sir Richard Monday died at Monday-place:
His lady's worth, his daughter's we peruse,
And find his grandsons all as rich as Jews:
He gave reforming charities a sum,
And bought the blessing of the blind and dumb;
Bequeathed to missions money from the stocks,
And Bibles issued from his private box;
But to his native place severely just,
He left a pittance bound in rigid trust; –
Two paltry pounds, on every quarter's-day,
(At church produced) for forty loaves should pay;
A stinted gift, that to the parish shows
He kept in mind their bounty and their blows!

from Marriages

　　Now to be wed a well-match'd couple came;
Twice had old Lodge been tied, and twice the dame;
Tottering they came and toying, (odious scene!)
And fond and simple, as they'd always been.
Children from wedlock we by laws restrain;
Why not prevent them, when they're such again?
Why not forbid the doting souls, to prove
Th' indecent fondling of preposterous love?
In spite of prudence, uncontroll'd by shame,
The amorous senior woos the toothless dame,
Relating idly, at the closing eve,
The youthful follies he disdains to leave;
Till youthful follies wake a transient fire,
When arm in arm they totter and retire.
　　So a fond pair of solemn birds, all day,

Blink in their seat and doze the hours away;
Then by the moon awaken'd, forth they move,
And fright the songsters with their cheerless love.
   So two sere trees, dry, stunted, and unsound,
Each other catch, when dropping to the ground;
Entwine their wither'd arms 'gainst wind and weather,
And shake their leafless heads and drop together.
   So two cold limbs, touch'd by Galvani's wire,
Move with new life, and feel awaken'd fire;
Quivering awhile, their flaccid forms remain,
Then turn to cold torpidity again.

from Burials

   Next died the Widow Goe, an active dame,
Famed ten miles round, and worthy all her fame;
She lost her husband when their loves were young,
But kept her farm, her credit and her tongue:
Full thirty years she ruled, with matchless skill,
With guiding judgment and resistless will;
Advice she scorn'd, rebellions she suppress'd,
And sons and servants bow'd at her behest.
Like that great man's, who to his Saviour came,
Were the strong words of this commanding dame; –
'Come,' if she said, they came: if 'go,' were gone;
And if 'do this,' – that instant it was done:
Her maidens told she was all eye and ear,
In darkness saw and could at distance hear; –
No parish-business in the place could stir,
Without direction or assent from her;
In turn she took each office as it fell,
Knew all their duties, and discharged them well;
The lazy vagrants in her presence shook,

And pregnant damsels fear'd her stern rebuke;
She look'd on want with judgment clear and cool,
And felt with reason and bestow'd by rule;
She match'd both sons and daughters to her mind,
And lent them eyes, for Love, she heard, was blind;
Yet ceaseless still she throve alert, alive,
The working bee, in full or empty hive;
Busy and carefull, like that working bee,
No time for love nor tender cares had she;
But when our farmers made their amorous vows,
She talk'd of market-steeds and patent-ploughs.
Not unemploy'd her evenings pass'd away,
Amusement closed, as business waked the day;
When to her toilet's brief concern she ran,
And conversation with her friends began,
Who all were welcome, what they saw, to share;
And joyous neighbours praised her Christmas fare,
That none around might, in their scorn, complain
Of Gossip Goe as greedy in her gain.
    Thus long she reign'd, admired, if not approved;
Praised, if not honour'd; fear'd, if not beloved; –
When, as the busy days of Spring drew near,
That call'd for all the forecast of the year;
When lively hope the rising crops survey'd,
And April promised what September paid;
When stray'd her lambs where gorse and greenweed grow;
When rose her grass in richer vales below;
When pleased she look'd on all the smiling land,
And viewed the hinds, who wrought at her command;
(Poultry in groups still follow'd where she went;)
Then dread o'ercame her, – that her days were spent.
    'Bless me! I die, and not a warning giv'n, –
With *much* to do on Earth, and ALL for Heav'n! –
No reparation for my soul's affairs,
No leave petition'd for the barn's repairs;

Accounts perplex'd, my interest yet unpaid,
My mind unsettled, and my will unmade; –
A lawyer haste, and in your way, a priest;
And let me die in one good work at least.'
She spake, and, trembling, dropp'd upon her knees,
Heaven in her eye and in her hand her keys;
And still the more she found her life decay,
With greater force she grasp'd those signs of sway:
Then fell and died! – In haste her sons drew near,
And dropp'd, in haste, the tributary tear,
Then from th' adhering clasp the keys unbound,
And consolation for their sorrow found.

from Sir Eustace Grey

Then was I cast from out my state;
   Two fiends of darkness led my way;
They waked me early, watch'd me late,
   My dread by night, my plague by day!
Oh! I was made their sport, their play,
   Through many a stormy troubled year;
And how they used their passive prey
   Is sad to tell: – but you shall hear.

And first, before they sent me forth,
   Through this unpitying world to run,
They robb'd Sir Eustace of his worth,
   Lands, manors, lordships, every one;
So was that gracious man undone,
   Was spurn'd as vile, was scorn'd as poor,
Whom every former friend would shun,
   And menials drove from every door.

Then those ill-favour'd Ones, whom none
   But my unhappy eyes could view,
Led me, with wild emotion, on,
   And, with resistless terror, drew.
Through lands we fled, o'er seas we flew,
   And halted on a boundless plain;
Where nothing fed, nor breathed, nor grew,
   But silence ruled the still domain.

Upon that boundless plain, below,
   The setting sun's last rays were shed,

And gave a mild and sober glow,
    Where all were still, asleep, or dead;
Vast ruins in the midst were spread,
    Pillars and pediments sublime,
Where the grey moss had form'd a bed,
    And clothed the crumbling spoils of time.

There was I fix'd, I know not how,
    Condemn'd for untold years to stay:
Yet years were not; – one dreadful *now*
    Endured no change of night or day;
The same mild evening's sleeping ray
    Shone softly-solemn and serene,
And all that time I gazed away,
    The setting sun's sad rays were seen.

At length a moment's sleep stole on, –
    Again came my commission'd foes;
Again through sea and land we're gone,
    No peace, no respite, no repose:
Above the dark broad sea we rose,
    We ran through bleak and frozen land;
I had no strength their strength t' oppose,
    An infant in a giant's hand.

They placed me where those streamers play,
    Those nimble beams of brilliant light;
It would the stoutest heart dismay,
    To see, to feel, that dreadful sight:
So swift, so pure, so cold, so bright,
    They pierced my frame with icy wound,
And all that half-year's polar night,
    Those dancing streamers wrapp'd me round.

Slowly that darkness pass'd away,
    When down upon the earth I fell, –
Some hurried sleep was mine by day;
    But, soon as toll'd the evening bell,
They forced me on, where ever dwell
    Far-distant men in cities fair,
Cities of whom no trav'lers tell,
    Nor feet but mine were wanderers there.

Their watchmen stare, and stand aghast,
    As on we hurry through the dark;
The watch-light blinks as we go past,
    The watch-dog shrinks and fears to bark;
The watch-tower's bell sounds shrill; and, hark!
    The free wind blows – we've left the town –
A wide sepulchral-ground I mark,
    And on a tombstone place me down.

What monuments of mighty dead!
    What tombs of various kinds are found!
And stones erect their shadows shed
    On humble graves, with wickers bound;
Some risen fresh, above the ground,
    Some level with the native clay,
What sleeping millions wait the sound,
    'Arise, ye dead, and come away!'

Alas! they stay not for that call;
    Spare me this wo! ye demons, spare! –
They come! the shrouded shadows all, –
    'Tis more than mortal brain can bear;
Rustling they rise, they sternly glare
    At man upheld by vital breath;
Who, led by wicked fiends, should dare
    To join the shadowy troops of death!

Yes, I have felt all man can feel,
  Till he shall pay his nature's debt;
Ills that no hope has strength to heal,
  No mind the comfort to forget:
Whatever cares the heart can fret,
  The spirits wear, the temper gall,
Wo, want, dread, anguish, all beset
  My sinful soul! – together all!

Those fiends upon a shaking fen
  Fix'd me, in dark tempestuous night,
There never trod the foot of men,
  There flock'd the fowl in wint'ry flight;
There danced the moor's deceitful light
  Above the pool where sedges grow;
And when the morning-sun shone bright,
  It shone upon a field of snow.

They hung me on a bough so small,
  The rook could build her nest no higher;
They fix'd me on the trembling ball
  That crowns the steeple's quiv'ring spire;
They set me where the seas retire,
  But drown with their returning tide;
And made me flee the mountain's fire,
  When rolling from its burning side.

I've hung upon the ridgy steep
  Of cliffs, and held the rambling brier;
I've plunged below the billowy deep,
  Where air was sent me to respire;
I've been where hungry wolves retire;
  And (to complete my woes) I've ran
Where Bedlam's crazy crew conspire
  Against the life of reasoning man.

I've furl'd in storms the flapping sail,
  By hanging from the topmast-head;
I've served the vilest slaves in jail,
  And pick'd the dunghill's spoil for bread;
I've made the badger's hole my bed,
  I've wander'd with a gipsy crew;
I've dreaded all the guilty dread,
  And done what they would fear to do.

On sand, where ebbs and flows the flood,
  Midway they placed and bade me die;
Propp'd on my staff, I stoutly stood
  When the swift waves came rolling by;
And high they rose, and still more high,
  Till my lips drank the bitter brine;
I sobb'd convulsed, then cast mine eye,
  And saw the tide's re-flowing sign.

And then, my dreams were such as nought
  Could yield but my unhappy case;
I've been of thousand devils caught,
  And thrust into that horrid place.
Where reign dismay, despair, disgrace;
  Furies with iron fangs were there,
To torture that accursed race,
  Doom'd to dismay, disgrace, despair.

The Borough

from General Description

   Be it the summer-noon: a sandy space
The ebbing tide has left upon its place;
Then just the hot and stony beach above,
Light twinkling streams in bright confusion move;
(For heated thus, the warmer air ascends,
And with the cooler in its fall contends) –
Then the broad bosom of the ocean keeps
An equal motion; swelling as it sleeps,
Then slowly sinking; curling to the strand,
Faint, lazy waves o'ercreep the ridgy sand,
On tap the tarry boat with gentle blow,
And back return in silence, smooth and slow.
Ships in the calm seem anchor'd; for they glide
On the still sea, urged solely by the tide;
Art thou not present, this calm scene before,
Where all beside is pebbly length of shore,
And far as eye can reach, it can discern no more?
   Yet sometimes comes a ruffling cloud to make
The quiet surface of the ocean shake;
As an awaken'd giant with a frown
Might show his wrath, and then to sleep sink down.
   View now the winter-storm! above, one cloud,
Black and unbroken, all the skies o'ershroud;
Th' unwieldy porpoise through the day before
Had roll'd in view of boding men on shore;
And sometimes hid and sometimes show'd his form,
Dark as the cloud, and furious as the storm.
   All where the eye delights, yet dreads to roam,
The breaking billows cast the flying foam

Upon the billows rising – all the deep
Is restless change; the waves so swell'd and steep,
Breaking and sinking, and the sunken swells,
Nor one, one moment, in its station dwells:
But nearer land you may the billows trace,
As if contending in their watery chase;
May watch the mightiest till the shoal they reach,
Then break and hurry to their utmost stretch;
Curl'd as they come, they strike with furious force,
And then re-flowing, take their grating course,
Raking the rounded flints, which ages past
Roll'd by their rage, and shall to ages last.
    Far off the petrel in the troubled way
Swims with her brood, or flutters in the spray;
She rises often, often drops again,
And sports at ease on the tempestuous main.
    High o'er the restless deep, above the reach
Of gunner's hope, vast flights of wild-ducks stretch;
Far as the eye can glance on either side,
In a broad space and level line they glide;
All in their wedge-like figures from the north,
Day after day, flight after flight, go forth.
    In-shore their passage tribes of sea-gulls urge,
And drop for prey within the sweeping surge;
Oft in the rough opposing blast they fly
Far back, then turn, and all their force apply,
While to the storm they give their weak complaining cry;
Or clap the sleek white pinion to the breast,
And in the restless ocean dip for rest.

from The Church

Enter'd the Church; we to a tomb proceed,
Whose names and titles few attempt to read;
Old English letters, and those half pick'd out,
Leave us, unskilful readers, much in doubt;
Our sons shall see its more degraded state;
The tomb of grandeur hastens to its fate;
That marble arch, our sexton's favourite show,
With all those ruff'd and painted pairs below;
The noble lady and the lord who rest
Supine, as courtly dame and warrior dress'd;
All are departed from their state sublime,
Mangled and wounded in their war with time
Colleagued with mischief; here a leg is fled,
And lo! the baron with but half a head;
Midway is cleft the arch; the very base
Is batter'd round and shifted from its place.
    Wonder not, mortal, at thy quick decay –
See! men of marble piece-meal melt away;
When whose the image we no longer read,
But monuments themselves memorials need.

from Law

    The trader, grazier, merchant, priest and all,
Whose sons aspiring, to professions call,
Choose from their lads some bold and subtle boy,
And judge him fitted for this grave employ:
Him a keen old practitioner admits,
To write five years and exercise his wits:
The youth has heard – it is in fact his creed –
Mankind dispute, that lawyers may be fee'd:

Jails, bailiffs, writs, all terms and threats of law,
Grow now familiar as once top and taw;
Rage, hatred, fear, the mind's severer ills,
All bring employment, all augment his bills:
As feels the surgeon for the mangled limb,
The mangled mind is but a job for him;
Thus taught to think, these legal reasoners draw
Morals and maxims from their views of law;
They cease to judge by precepts taught in schools,
By man's plain sense, or by religious rules;
No! nor by law itself, in truth discern'd,
But as its statutes may be warp'd and turn'd:
How should they judge of man, his word and deed,
They in their books and not their bosoms read:
Of some good act you speak with just applause,
'No! no!' says he, ''twould be a losing cause:'
Blame you some tyrant's deed? – he answers 'Nay,
He'll get a verdict; heed you what you say.'
Thus to conclusions from examples led,
The heart resigns all judgment to the head;
Law, law alone for ever kept in view,
His measures guides, and rules his conscience too;
Of ten commandments, he confesses three
Are yet in force, and tells you which they be,
As law instructs him, thus: 'Your neighbour's wife
You must not take, his chattels, nor his life;
Break these decrees, for damage you must pay;
These you must reverence, and the rest – you may.'

  Law was design'd to keep a state in peace;
To punish robbery, that wrong might cease;
To be impregnable; a constant fort,
To which the weak and injured might resort:
But these perverted minds its force employ,
Not to protect mankind, but to annoy;
And long as ammunition can be found,

Its lightning flashes and its thunders sound.
   Or law with lawyers in an ample still,
Wrought by the passions' heat with chymic skill;
While the fire burns, the gains are quickly made,
And freely flow the profits of the trade;
Nay, when the fierceness fails, these artists blow
The dying fire, and make the embers glow,
As long as they can make the smaller profits flow;
At length the process of itself will stop,
When they perceive they've drawn out every drop.

from Trades

   There is my friend the Weaver; strong desires
Reign in his breast; 'tis beauty he admires:
See! to the shady grove he wings his way,
And feels in hope the raptures of the day –
Eager he looks; and soon, to glad his eyes,
From the sweet bower, by nature form'd, arise
Bright troops of virgin moths and fresh-born butterflies;
Who broke that morning from their half-year's sleep,
To fly o'er flow'rs where they were wont to creep.
   Above the sovereign oak, a sovereign skims,
The purple emp'ror, strong in wing and limbs:
There fair Camilla takes her flight serene,
Adonis blue, and Paphia silver-queen;
With every filmy fly from mead or bower,
And hungry Sphinx who threads the honey'd flower;
She o'er the Larkspur's bed, where sweets abound,
Views ev'ry bell, and hums th' approving sound;
Poised on her busy plumes, with feeling nice
She draws from every flower, nor tries a floret twice.

from Amusements

Now is it pleasant in the summer-eve,
When a broad shore retiring waters leave,
Awhile to wait upon the firm fair sand,
When all is calm at sea, all still at land;
And there the ocean's produce to explore,
As floating by, or rolling on the shore;
Those living jellies which the flesh inflame,
Fierce as a nettle, and from that its name;
Some in huge masses, some that you may bring
In the small compass of a lady's ring;
Figured by hand divine – there's not a gem
Wrought by man's art to be compared to them;
Soft, brilliant, tender, through the wave they glow,
And make the moonbeam brighter where they flow.
Involved in sea-wrack, here you find a race,
Which science doubting, knows not where to place;
On shell or stone is dropp'd the embryo-seed,
And quickly vegetates a vital breed.

While thus with pleasing wonder you inspect
Treasures the vulgar in their scorn reject,
See as they float along th' entangled weeds
Slowly approach, upborne on bladdery beads;
Wait till they land, and you shall then behold
The fiery sparks those tangled frons' infold,
Myriads of living points; th' unaided eye
Can but the fire and not the form descry.
And now your view upon the ocean turn,
And there the splendour of the waves discern;
Cast but a stone, or strike them with an oar,
And you shall flames within the deep explore;
Or scoop the stream phosphoric as you stand,
And the cold flames shall flash along your hand;

When, lost in wonder, you shall walk and gaze
On weeds that sparkle, and on waves that blaze.
　The ocean too has winter-views serene,
When all you see through densest fog is seen;
When you can hear the fishers near at hand
Distinctly speak, yet see not where they stand;
Or sometimes them and not their boat discern,
Or half-conceal'd some figure at the stern;
The view's all bounded, and from side to side
Your utmost prospect but a few ells wide;
Boys who, on shore, to sea the pebble cast,
Will hear it strike against the viewless mast;
While the stern boatman growls his fierce disdain,
At whom he knows not, whom he threats in vain.
　'Tis pleasant then to view the nets float past,
Net after net till you have seen the last;
And as you wait till all beyond you slip,
A boat comes gliding from an anchor'd ship,
Breaking the silence with the dipping oar,
And their own tones, as labouring for the shore;
Those measured tones which with the scene agree,
And give a sadness to serenity.

from Inns

　Third in our Borough's list appears the sign
Of a fair queen – the gracious Caroline;
But in decay – each feature in the face
Has stain of Time, and token of disgrace.
The storm of winter, and the summer-sun,
Have on that form their equal mischief done;
The features now are all disfigured seen,
And not one charm adorns th' insulted queen:

To this poor face was never paint applied,
Th' unseemly work of cruel Time to hide;
Here we may rightly such neglect upbraid,
Paint on such faces is by prudence laid.
Large the domain, but all within combine
To correspond with the dishonour'd sign;
And all around dilapidates; you call –
But none replies – they're inattentive all:
At length a ruin'd stable holds your steed,
While you through large and dirty rooms proceed,
Spacious and cold; a proof they once had been
In honour – now magnificently mean;
Till in some small half-furnish'd room you rest,
Whose dying fire denotes it had a guest.
In those you pass'd where former splendour reign'd,
You saw the carpets torn, the paper stain'd;
Squares of discordant glass in windows fix'd,
And paper oil'd in many a space betwixt;
A soil'd and broken sconce, a mirror crack'd,
With table underpropp'd, and chairs new-back'd;
A marble side-slab with ten thousand stains,
And all an ancient tavern's poor remains.
  With much entreaty, they your food prepare,
And acid wine afford, with meagre fare;
Heartless you sup; and when a dozen times
You've read the fractured window's senseless rhymes;
Have been assured that Phoebe Green was fair,
And Peter Jackson took his supper there;
You reach a chilling chamber, where you dread,
Damps, hot or cold, from a tremendous bed;
Late comes your sleep, and you are waken'd soon
By rustling tatters of the old festoon.

from Players

Peruse these bills, and see what each can do, –
Behold! the prince, the slave, the monk, the Jew;
Change but the garment, and they'll all engage
To take each part, and act in every age:
Cull'd from all houses, what a house are they!
Swept from all barns, our borough-critics say;
But with some portion of a critic's ire,
We all endure them; there are some admire.
They might have praise, confined to farce alone;
Full well they grin, they should not try to groan;
But then our servants' and our seamen's wives
Love all that rant and rapture as their lives;
He who 'Squire Richard's part could well sustain,
Finds as King Richard he must roar amain –
'My horse! my horse!' Low! now to their abodes,
Come lords and lovers, empresses and gods.
The master-mover of these scenes has made
No trifling gain in this adventurous trade;
Trade we may term it, for he duly buys
Arms out of use and undirected eyes;
These he instructs, and guides them as he can,
And vends each night the manufactured man:
Long as our custom lasts, they gladly stay,
Then strike their tents, like Tartars! and away!
The place grows bare where they too long remain,
But grass will rise ere they return again.
    Children of Thespis, welcome! knights and queens!
Counts! barons! beauties! when before your scenes,
And mighty monarchs thund'ring from your throne;
Then step behind, and all your glory's gone:
Of crown and palace, throne and guards bereft,
The pomp is vanish'd and the care is left.

Yet strong and lively is the joy they feel,
When the full house secures the plenteous meal;
Flatt'ring and flatter'd, each attempts to raise
A brother's merits for a brother's praise:
For never hero shows a prouder heart,
Than he who proudly acts a hero's part;
Nor without cause; the boards, we know, can yield
Place for fierce contest, like the tented field.

   Graceful to tread the stage, to be in turn
The prince we honour, and the knave we spurn;
Bravely to bear the tumult of the crowd,
The hiss tremendous, and the censure loud:
These are their parts, – and he who these sustains
Deserves some praise and profit for his pains.
Heroes at least of gentler kind are they,
Against whose swords no weeping widows pray,
No blood their fury sheds, nor havoc marks their way.

   Sad happy race! soon raised and soon depress'd,
Your days all pass'd in jeopardy and jest;
Poor without prudence, with afflictions vain,
Not warn'd by misery, not enrich'd by gain;
Whom justice pitying, chides from place to place,
A wandering, careless, wretched, merry race,
Who cheerful looks assume, and play the parts
Of happy rovers with repining hearts;
Then cast off care, and in the mimic pain
Of tragic wo, feel spirits light and vain,
Distress and hope – the mind's, the body's wear,
The man's affliction, and the actor's tear:
Alternate times of fasting and excess
Are yours, ye smiling children of distress.

from Inhabitants of the Alms-House

We had a sprightly nymph – in every town
Are some such sprights, who wander up and down;
She had her useful arts, and could contrive,
In time's despite, to stay at twenty-five; –
'Here will I rest; move on, thou lying year,
This is mine age, and I will rest me here.'
    Arch was her look, and she had pleasant ways
Your good opinion of her heart to raise;
Her speech was lively, and with ease express'd,
And well she judged the tempers she address'd:
If some soft stripling had her keenness felt,
She knew the way to make his anger melt;
Wit was allow'd her, though but few could bring
Direct example of a witty thing;
'Twas that gay, pleasant, smart, engaging speech,
Her beaux admired, and just within their reach;
Not indiscreet perhaps, but yet more free
Than prudish nymphs allow their wit to be.
    Novels and plays, with poems, old and new,
Were all the books our nymph attended to;
Yet from the press no treatise issued forth,
But she would speak precisely of its worth.
    She with the London stage familiar grew,
And every actor's name and merit knew;
She told how this or that their part mistook,
And of the rival Romeos gave the look;
Of either house 'twas hers the strength to see,
Then judge with candour – 'Drury-Lane for me.'
    What made this knowledge, what this skill complete?
A fortnight's visit in Whitechapel-street.
    Her place in life was rich and poor between,
With those a favourite, and with these a queen;

She could her parts assume, and condescend
To friends more humble while an humble friend;
And thus a welcome, lively guest could pass,
Threading her pleasant way from class to class.
  'Her reputation?' – That was like her wit,
And seem'd her manner and her state to fit;
Something there was, what, none presumed to say,
Clouds lightly passing on a smiling day. –
Whispers and hints which went from ear to ear,
And mix'd reports no judge on earth could clear.

from The Poor and Their Dwellings

  Lo! yonder shed; observe its garden-ground,
With the low paling, form'd of wreck, around:
There dwells a fisher; if you view his boat,
With bed and barrel – 'tis his house afloat;
Look at his house, where ropes, nets, blocks abound,
Tar, pitch, and oakum – 'tis his boat aground:
That space enclosed, but little he regards,
Spread o'er with relics of masts, sails, and yards:
Fish by the wall, on spit of elder, rest,
Of all his food, the cheapest and the best,
By his own labour caught, for his own hunger dress'd.
  Here our reformers come not; none object
To paths polluted, or upbraid neglect;
None care that ashy heaps at doors are cast,
That coal-dust flies along the blinding blast:
None heed the stagnant pools on either side,
Where new-launch'd ships of infant sailors ride:
Rodneys in rags here British valour boast,
And lisping Nelsons fright the Gallic coast.
They fix the rudder, set the swelling sail,

They point the bowsprit, and they blow the gale:
True to her port, the frigate scuds away,
And o'er that frowning ocean finds her bay:
Her owner rigg'd her, and he knows her worth,
And sees her, fearless, gunwale-deep go forth;
Dreadless he views his sea, by breezes curl'd,
When inch-high billows vex the watery world.

The Parish Clerk

With our late vicar, and his age the same,
His clerk, hight Jachin, to his office came;
The like slow speech was his, the like tall slender frame:
But Jachin was the gravest man on ground,
And heard his master's jokes with look profound;
For worldly wealth this man of letters sigh'd,
And had a sprinkling of the spirit's pride:
But he was sober, chaste, devout, and just,
One whom his neighbours could believe and trust:
Of none suspected, neither man nor maid
By him were wrong'd, or were of him afraid.

There was indeed a frown, a trick of state
In Jachin; – formal was his air and gait;
But if he seem'd more solemn and less kind
Then some light men to light affairs confined,
Still 'twas allow'd that he should so behave
As in high seat, and be severely grave.

This book-taught man, to man's first foe profess'd
Defiance stern, and hate that knew not rest;
He held that Satan, since the world began,
In every act, had strife with every man;
That never evil deed on earth was done,
But of the acting parties he was one;

The flattering guide to make ill prospects clear;
To smooth rough ways the constant pioneer;
The ever-tempting, soothing, softening power,
Ready to cheat, seduce, deceive, devour.

'Me has the sly seducer oft withstood,'
Said pious Jachin, – 'but he gets no good;
I pass the house where swings the tempting sign,
And pointing, tell him, 'Satan, that is thine:'
I pass the damsels pacing down the street,
And look more grave and solemn when we meet;
Nor doth it irk me to rebuke their smiles,
Their wanton ambling and their watchful wiles:
Nay, like the good John Bunyan, when I view
Those forms, I'm angry at the ills they do;
That I could pinch and spoil, in sin's despite,
Beauties! which frail and evil thoughts excite.

'At feasts and banquets seldom am I found,
And (save at church) abhor a tuneful sound;
To plays and shows I run not to and fro,
And where my master goes forbear to go.'

No wonder Satan took the thing amiss,
To be opposed by such a man as this –
A man so grave, important, cautious, wise,
Who dared not trust his feeling or his eyes;

No wonder he should lurk and lie in wait,
Should fit his hooks and ponder on his bait,
Should on his movements keep a watchful eye;
For he pursued a fish who led the fry.

With his own peace our clerk was not content,
He tried, good man! to make his friends repent.
'Nay, nay, my friends, from inns and taverns fly;
You may suppress your thirst, but not supply:
A foolish proverb says, 'the devil's at home;'
But he is there, and tempts in every room:
Men feel, they know not why, such places please;

His are the spells – they're idleness and ease;
Magic of fatal kind he throws around,
Where care is banish'd but the heart is bound.
  'Think not of beauty; when a maid you meet,
Turn from her view and step across the street;
Dread all the sex: their looks create a charm,
A smile should fright you and a word alarm:
E'en I myself, with all my watchful care,
Have for an instant felt th' insidious snare,
And caught my sinful eyes at th' endangering stare;
Till I was forced to smite my bounding breast
With forceful blow and bid the bold-one rest.
  'Go not with crowds when they to pleasure run,
But public joy in private safety shun:
When bells, diverted from their true intent,
Ring loud for some deluded mortal sent
To hear or make long speech in parliament;
What time the many, that unruly beast,
Roars its rough joy and shares the final feast:
Then heed my counsel, shut thine ears and eyes;
A few will hear me – for the few are wise.'
  Not Satan's friends, nor Satan's self could bear
The cautious man who took of souls such care;
An interloper, – one who out of place,
Had volunteer'd upon the side of grace:
There was his master ready once a week
To give advice; what further need he seek?
'Amen, so be it:' – what had he to do
With more than this? – 'twas insolent and new;
And some determined on a way to see
How frail he was, that so it might not be.
  First they essay'd to tempt our saint to sin,
By points of doctrine argued at an inn;
Where he might warmly reason, deeply drink,
Then lose all power to argue and to think.

In vain they tried; he took the question up,
Clear'd every doubt, and barely touch'd the cup:
By many a text he proved his doctrine sound,
And look'd in triumph on the tempters round.
    Next 'twas their care an artful lass to find,
Who might consult him, as perplex'd in mind;
She they conceived might put her case with fears,
With tender tremblings and seducing tears;
She might such charms of various kind display,
That he would feel their force and melt away:
For why of nymphs such caution and such dread,
Unless he felt and fear'd to be misled?
    She came, she spake: he calmly heard her case,
And plainly told her 'twas a want of grace;
Bade her 'such fancies and affections check,
And wear a thicker muslin on her neck.'
Abased, his human foes the combat fled,
And the stern clerk yet higher held his head.
They were indeed a weak, impatient set,
But their shrewd prompter had his engines yet;
Had various means to make a mortal trip,
Who shunn'd a flowing bowl and rosy lip;
And knew a thousand ways his heart to move,
Who flies from banquets and who laughs at love.
    Thus far the playful Muse has lent her aid,
But now departs, of graver theme afraid;
Her may we seek in more appropriate time, –
There is no jesting with distress and crime.
    Our worthy clerk had now arrived at fame,
Such as but few in his degree might claim;
But he was poor, and wanted not the sense
That lowly rates the praise without the pence:
He saw the common herd with reverence treat
The weakest burgess whom they chanced to meet;
While few respected his exalted views,

And all beheld his doublet and his shoes:
None, when they meet, would to his parts allow
(Save his poor boys) a hearing or a bow:
To this false judgment of the vulgar mind,
He was not fully, as a saint, resign'd;
He found it much his jealous soul affect,
To fear derision and to find neglect.

The year was bad, the christening-fees were small,
The weddings few, the parties paupers all:
Desire of gain with fear of want combined,
Raised sad commotion in his wounded mind;
Wealth was in all his thoughts, his views, his dreams,
And prompted base desires and baseless schemes.

Alas! how often erring mortals keep
The strongest watch against the foes who sleep;
While the more wakeful, bold and artful foe
Is suffer'd guardless and unmark'd to go.

Once in a month the sacramental bread
Our clerk with wine upon the table spread;
The custom this, that, as the vicar reads,
He for our off'rings round the church proceeds:
Tall spacious seats the wealthier people hid,
And none had view of what his neighbour did;
Laid on the box and mingled when they fell,
Who should the worth of each oblation tell?
Now as poor Jachin took the usual round,
And saw the alms and heard the metal sound,
He had a thought; – at first it was no more
Than – 'these have cash and give it to the poor:'
A second thought from this to work began –
'And can they give it to a poorer man?'
Proceeding thus, – 'My merit could they know,
And knew my need, how freely they'd bestow;
But though they know not, these remain the same;
And are a strong, although a secret claim:

To me, alas! the want and worth are known,
Why then, in fact, 'tis but to take my own.'
   Thought after thought pour'd in, a tempting train, –
'Suppose it done, – who is it could complain?
How could the poor? for they such trifles share,
As add no comfort, as suppress no care;
But many a pittance makes a worthy heap, –
What says the law? that silence puts to sleep: –
Nought then forbids, the danger could we shun,
And sure the business may be safely done.
   'But am I earnest? – earnest? No. – I say,
If such my mind, that I could plan a way;
Let me reflect; – I've not allow'd me time
To purse the pieces, and if dropp'd they'd chime:'
Fertile is evil in the soul of man, –
He paused, – said Jachin, 'They may drop on bran.
Why then 'tis safe and (all consider'd) just,
The poor receive it, – 'tis no breach of trust
The old and widows may their trifles miss,
There must be evil in a good like this:
But I'll be kind – the sick I'll visit twice,
When now but once, and freely give advice.
Yet let me think again:' – Again he tried,
For stronger reasons on his passion's side,
And quickly these were found, yet slowly he complied.
   The morning came: the common service done, –
Shut every door, – the solemn rite begun, –
And, as the priest the sacred sayings read,
The clerk went forward, trembling as he tread;
O'er the tall pew he held the box, and heard
The offer'd piece, rejoicing as he fear'd:
Just by the pillar, as he cautious tripp'd
And turn'd the aile, he then a portion shipp'd
From the full store, and to the pocket sent,
But held a moment – and then down it went.

The priest read on, on walk'd the man afraid,
Till a gold offering in the plate was laid;
Trembling he took it, for a moment stopp'd,
Then down it fell, and sounded as it dropp'd;
Amazed he started, for th' affrighted man,
Lost and bewilder'd, thought not of the bran;
But all were silent, all on things intent
Of high concern, none ear to money lent;
So on he walk'd, more cautious than before,
And gain'd the purposed sum and one piece more.

 Practice makes perfect; when the month came round,
He dropp'd the cash, nor listen'd for a sound;
But yet, when last of all th' assembled flock,
He ate and drank, – it gave th' electric shock:
Oft was he forced his reasons to repeat,
Ere he could kneel in quiet at his seat;
But custom soothed him – ere a single year
All this was done without restraint or fear:
Cool and collected, easy and composed,
He was correct till all the service closed;
Then to his home, without a groan or sigh,
Gravely he went, and laid his treasure by.

 Want will complain: some widows had express'd
A doubt if they were favour'd like the rest;
The rest described with like regret their dole,
And thus from parts they reason'd to the whole;
When all agreed some evil must be done,
Or rich men's hearts grew harder than a stone.

 Our easy vicar cut the matter short;
He would not listen to such vile report.

 All were not thus – there govern'd in that year
A stern stout churl, an angry overseer;
A tyrant fond of power, loud, lewd, and most severe:
Him the mild vicar, him the graver clerk,
Advised, reproved, but nothing would he mark,

Save the disgrace, 'and that, my friends,' said he,
'Will I avenge, whenever time may be.'
And now, alas! 'twas time; – from man to man
Doubt and alarm and shrewd suspicions ran.

   With angry spirit and with sly intent,
This parish-ruler to the altar went;
A private mark he fix'd on shillings three,
And but one mark could in the money see;
Besides, in peering round, he chanced to note
A sprinkling slight on Jachin's Sunday-coat:
All doubt was over: – when the flock were bless'd,
In wrath he rose, and thus his mind express'd.

   'Foul deeds are here!' and saying this, he took
The clerk, whose conscience, in her cold-fit, shook:
His pocket then was emptied on the place;
All saw his guilt; all witness'd his disgrace:
He fell, he fainted, not a groan, a look,
Escaped the culprit; 'twas a final stroke –
A death-wound never to be heal'd – a fall
That all had witness'd, and amazed were all.

   As he recover'd, to his mind it came,
'I owe to Satan this disgrace and shame:'
All the seduction now appear'd in view;
'Let me withdraw,' he said, and he withdrew;
No one withheld him, all in union cried,
E'en the avenger, – 'We are satisfied:'
For what has death in any form to give,
Equal to that man's terrors, if he live?

   He lived in freedom, but he hourly saw
How much more fatal justice is than law;
He saw another in his office reign,
And his mild master treat him with disdain;
He saw that all men shunn'd him, some reviled,
The harsh pass'd frowning, and the simple smiled;
The town maintain'd him, but with some reproof,

'And clerks and scholars proudly kept aloof.'
  In each lone place, dejected and dismay'd,
Shrinking from view, his wasting form he laid;
Or to the restless sea and roaring wind
Gave the strong yearnings of a ruin'd mind:
On the broad beach, the silent summer-day,
Stretch'd on some wreck, he wore his life away;
Or where the river mingles with the sea,
Or on the mud-bank by the elder-tree,
Or by the bounding marsh-dyke, there was he:
And when unable to forsake the town,
In the blind courts he sate desponding down –
Always alone; then feebly would he crawl
The church-way walk, and lean upon the wall:
Too ill for this, he lay beside the door,
Compell'd to hear the reasoning of the poor:
He look'd so pale, so weak, the pitying crowd
Their firm belief of his repentance vow'd;
They saw him then so ghastly and so thin,
That they exclaim'd, 'Is this the work of sin?'
  'Yes,' in his better moments, he replied,
'Of sinful avarice and the spirit's pride; –
While yet untempted, I was safe and well;
Temptation came; I reason'd, and I fell:
To be man's guide and glory I design'd,
A rare example for our sinful kind;
But now my weakness and my guilt I see,
And am a warning – man, be warn'd by me!'
  He said, and saw no more the human face;
To a lone loft he went, his dying place,
And, as the vicar of his state inquired,
Turn'd to the wall and silently expired!

Peter Grimes

Old Peter Grimes made fishing his employ,
His wife he cabin'd with him and his boy,
And seem'd that life laborious to enjoy:
To town came quiet Peter with his fish,
And had of all a civil word and wish.
He left his trade upon the sabbath-day,
And took young Peter in his hand to pray:
But soon the stubborn boy from care broke loose,
At first refused, then added his abuse:
His father's love he scorn'd, his power defied,
But being drunk, wept sorely when he died.
Yes! then he wept, and to his mind there came
Much of his conduct, and he felt the shame, –
How he had oft the good old man reviled,
And never paid the duty of a child;
How, when the father in his Bible read,
He in contempt and anger left the shed:
'It is the word of life,' the parent cried;
– 'This is the life itself,' the boy replied;
And while old Peter in amazement stood,
Gave the hot spirit to his boiling blood: –
How he, with oath and furious speech, began
To prove his freedom and assert the man;
And when the parent check'd his impious rage,
How he had cursed the tyranny of age, –
Nay, once had dealt the sacrilegious blow
On his bare head, and laid his parent low;
The father groan'd – 'If thou art old,' said he,
'And hast a son – thou wilt remember me:
Thy mother left me in a happy time,

Thou kill'dst not her – Heav'n spares the double crime.'
   On an inn-settle, in his maudlin grief,
This he revolved, and drank for his relief.
Now lived the youth in freedom, but debarr'd
From constant pleasure, and he thought it hard;
Hard that he could not every wish obey,
But must awhile relinquish ale and play;
Hard! that he could not to his cards attend,
But must acquire the money he would spend.
With greedy eye, he look'd on all he saw,
He knew not justice, and he laugh'd at law;
On all he mark'd he stretch'd his ready hand;
He fish'd by water, and he filch'd by land:
Oft in the night has Peter dropp'd his oar,
Fled from his boat and sought for prey on shore;
Oft up the hedge-row glided, on his back
Bearing the orchard's produce in a sack,
Or farm-yard load, tugg'd fiercely from the stack;
And as these wrongs to greater numbers rose,
The more he look'd on all men as his foes.

   He built a mud-wall'd hovel, where he kept
His various wealth, and there he oft-times slept;
But no success could please his cruel soul,
He wish'd for one to trouble and control;
He wanted some obedient boy to stand
And bear the blow of his outrageous hand;
And hoped to find in some propitious hour
A feeling creature subject to his power.

   Peter had heard there were in London then, –
Still have they being! – workhouse-clearing men,
Who, undisturb'd by feelings just or kind,
Would parish-boys to needy tradesmen bind:
They in their want a trifling sum would take,
And toiling slaves of piteous orphans make.

   Such Peter sought, and when a lad was found,

The sum was dealt him, and the slave was bound.
Some few in town observed in Peter's trap
A boy, with jacket blue and woollen cap;
But none inquired how Peter used the rope,
Or what the bruise, that made the stripling stoop;
None could the ridges on his back behold,
None sought him shiv'ring in the winter's cold;
None put the question, – 'Peter, dost thou give
The boy his food? – What, man! the lad must live:
Consider, Peter, let the child have bread,
He'll serve thee better if he's stroked and fed.'
None reason'd thus – and some, on hearing cries,
Said calmly, 'Grimes is at his exercise.'
  Pinn'd, beaten, cold, pinch'd, threaten'd, and abused –
His efforts punish'd and his food refused, –
Awake tormented, – soon aroused from sleep, –
Struck if he wept, and yet compell'd to weep,
The trembling boy dropp'd down and strove to pray,
Received a blow, and trembling turn'd away,
Or sobb'd and hid his piteous face; – while he,
The savage master, grinn'd in horrid glee:
He'd now the power he ever loved to show,
A feeling being subject to his blow.
  Thus lived the lad, in hunger, peril, pain,
His tears despised, his supplications vain:
Compell'd by fear to lie, by need to steal,
His bed uneasy and unbless'd his meal,
For three sad years the boy his tortures bore,
And then his pains and trials were no more.
  'How died he, Peter?' when the people said,
He growl'd – 'I found him lifeless in his bed;
Then tried for softer tone, and sigh'd, 'Poor Sam is dead.'
Yet murmurs were there, and some questions ask'd, –
How he was fed, how punish'd, and how task'd?
Much they suspected, but they little proved,

And Peter pass'd untroubled and unmoved.
    Another boy with equal ease was found,
The money granted, and the victim bound;
And what his fate? – One night it chanced he fell
From the boat's mast and perish'd in her well,
Where fish were living kept, and where the boy
(So reason'd men) could not himself destroy: –
    'Yes! so it was,' said Peter, 'in his play,
(For he was idle both by night and day,)
He climb'd the main-mast and then fell below;' –
Then show'd his corpse and pointed to the blow:
'What said the jury?' – they were long in doubt,
But sturdy Peter faced the matter out:
So they dismiss'd him, saying at the time,
'Keep fast your hatchway when you've boys who climb.'
This hit the conscience, and he colour'd more
Than for the closest questions put before.
    Thus all his fears the verdict set aside,
And at the slave-shop Peter still applied.
    Then came a boy, of manners soft and mild, –
Our seamen's wives with grief beheld the child;
All thought (the poor themselves) that he was one
Of gentle blood, some noble sinner's son,
Who had belike, deceived some humble maid,
Whom he had first seduced and then betray'd: –
However this, he seem'd a gracious lad,
In grief submissive and with patience sad.
    Passive he labour'd, till his slender frame
Bent with his loads, and he at length was lame:
Strange that a frame so weak could bear so long
The grossest insult and the foulest wrong;
But there were causes – in the town they gave
Fire, food, and comfort, to the gentle slave;
And though stern Peter, with a cruel hand,
And knotted rope, enforced the rude command,

Yet he consider'd what he'd lately felt,
And his vile blows with selfish pity dealt.

   One day such draughts the cruel fisher made,
He could not vend them in his borough-trade,
But sail'd for London-mart: the boy was ill,
But ever humbled to his master's will;
And on the river, where they smoothly sail'd,
He strove with terror and awhile prevail'd,
But new to danger on the angry sea,
He clung affrighten'd to his master's knee:
The boat grew leaky and the wind was strong,
Rough was the passage and the time was long;
His liquor fail'd, and Peter's wrath arose, –
No more is known – the rest we must suppose,
Or learn of Peter; – Peter says, he 'spied
The stripling's danger and for harbour tried;
Meantime the fish, and then th' apprentice died.'

   The pitying women raised a clamour round,
And weeping said, 'Thou hast thy 'prentice drown'd.

   Now the stern man was summon'd to the hall,
To tell his tale before the burghers all:
He gave th' account; profess'd the lad he loved,
And kept his brazen features all unmoved.

   The mayor himself with tone severe replied, –
'Henceforth with thee shall never boy abide;
Hire thee a freeman, whom thou durst not beat,
But who, in thy despite, will sleep and eat:
Free thou art now! – again shouldst thou appear,
Thou'lt find thy sentence, like thy soul, severe.'

   Alas! for Peter not a helping hand,
So was he hated, could he now command;
Alone he row'd his boat, alone he cast
His nets beside, or made his anchor fast;
To hold a rope or hear a curse was none, –
He toil'd and rail'd; he groan'd and swore alone.

Thus by himself compell'd to live each day,
To wait for certain hours the tide's delay;
At the same times the same dull views to see,
The bounding marsh-bank and the blighted tree;
The water only, when the tides were high,
When low, the mud half-cover'd and half-dry;
The sun-burnt tar that blisters on the planks,
And bank-side stakes in their uneven ranks;
Heaps of entangled weeds that slowly float,
As the tide rolls by the impeded boat.
When tides were neap, and, in the sultry day,
Through the tall bounding mud-banks made their way,
Which on each side rose swelling, and below
The dark warm flood ran silently and slow;
There anchoring, Peter chose from man to hide,
There hang his head, and view the lazy tide
In its hot slimy channel slowly glide;
Where the small eels that left the deeper way
For the warm shore, within the shallows play;
Where gaping muscles, left upon the mud,
Slope their slow passage to the fallen flood; –
Here dull and hopeless he'd lie down and trace
How sidelong crabs had scrawl'd their crooked race;
Or sadly listen to the tuneless cry
Of fishing gull or clanging golden-eye;
What time the sea-birds to the marsh would come,
And the loud bittern, from the bull-rush home,
Gave from the salt-ditch side the bellowing boom:
He nursed the feelings these dull scenes produce,
And loved to stop beside the opening sluice;
Where the small stream, confined in narrow bound,
Ran with a dull, unvaried, sadd'ning sound;
Where all, presented to the eye or ear,
Oppress'd the soul with misery, grief, and fear.
Besides these objects, there were places three,

Which Peter seem'd with certain dread to see;
When he drew near them he would turn from each,
And loudly whistle till he pass'd the reach.*

A change of scene to him brought no relief;
In town, 'twas plain, men took him for a thief:
The sailors' wives would stop him in the street,
And say, 'Now, Peter, thou'st no boy to beat:'
Infants at play, when they perceived him, ran,
Warning each other – 'That's the wicked man:'
He growl'd an oath, and in an angry tone
Cursed the whole place and wish'd to be alone.

Alone he was, the same dull scenes in view,
And still more gloomy in his sight they grew;
Though man he hated, yet employ'd alone
At bootless labour, he would swear and groan,
Cursing the shoals that glided by the spot,
And gulls that caught them when his arts could not.

Cold nervous tremblings shook his study frame,
And strange disease – he couldn't say the name;
Wild were his dreams, and oft he rose in fright,
Waked by his view of horrors in the night, –
Horrors that would the sternest minds amaze,
Horrors that demons might be proud to raise:
And though he felt forsaken, grieved at heart,
To think he lived from all mankind apart;
Yet, if a man approach'd, in terrors he would start.

A winter pass'd since Peter saw the town,
And summer-lodgers were again come down;
These, idly curious, with their glasses spied
The ships in bay as anchor'd for the tide, –
The river's craft, – the bustle of the quay, –

*The reaches in a river are those parts which extend from point to point. Johnson has not the word precisely in this sense: but it is very common, and, I believe, used wheresoever a navigable river can be found in this country.

And sea-port views, which landmen love to see.
　　One, up the river, had a man and boat
Seen day by day, now anchor'd, now afloat;
Fisher he seem'd, yet used no net nor hook;
Of sea-fowl swimming by no heed he took,
But on the gliding waves still fix'd his lazy look:
At certain stations he would view the stream,
As if he stood bewilder'd in a dream,
Or that some power had chain'd him for a time,
To feel a curse or meditate on crime.
　　This known, some curious, some in pity went,
And others question'd – 'Wretch, dost thou repent?
He heard, he trembled, and in fear resign'd
His boat: new terror fill'd his restless mind;
Furious he grew, and up the country ran,
And there they seized him – a distemper'd man: –
Him we received, and to a parish-bed,
Follow'd and cursed, the groaning man was led.
　　Here when they saw him, whom they used to shun,
A lost, lone man, so harass'd and undone;
Our gentle females, ever prompt to feel,
Perceived compassion on their anger steal;
His crimes they could not from their memories blot,
But they were grieved, and trembled at his lot.
　　A priest too came, to whom his words are told;
And all the signs they shudder'd to behold.
　　'Look! look!' they cried; 'his limbs with horror shake,
And as he grinds his teeth, what noise they make!
How glare his angry eyes, and yet he's not awake:
See! what cold drops upon his forehead stand,
And how he clenches that broad bony hand.'
　　The priest attending, found he spoke at times
As one alluding to his fears and crimes:
'It was the fall,' he mutter'd, 'I can show
The manner how – I never struck a blow:' –

And then aloud – 'Unhand me, free my chain;
On oath, he fell – it struck him to the brain: –
Why ask my father? – that old man will swear
Against my life; besides, he wasn't there: –
What, all agreed? – Am I to die to-day? –
My Lord, in mercy, give me time to pray.'

   Then, as they watch'd him, calmer he became,
And grew so weak he couldn't move his frame,
But murmuring spake, – while they could see and hear
The start of terror and the groan of fear;
See the large dew-beads on his forehead rise,
And the cold death-drop glaze his sunken eyes;
Nor yet he died, but with unwonted force
Seem'd with some fancied being to discourse:
He knew not us, or with accustom'd art
He hid the knowledge, yet exposed his heart;
'Twas part confession and the rest defence,
A madman's tale, with gleams of waking sense.

   'I'll tell you all,' he said, 'the very day
When the old man first placed them in my way:
My father's spirit – he who always tried
To give me trouble, when he lived and died –
When he was gone, he could not be content
To see my days in painful labour spent,
But would appoint his meetings, and he made
Me watch at these, and so neglect my trade.

   ''Twas one hot noon, all silent, still, serene,
No living being had I lately seen;
I paddled up and down and dipp'd my net,
But (such his pleasure) I could nothing get, –
A father's pleasure, when his toil was done,
To plague and torture thus an only son!
And so I sat and look'd upon the stream,
How it ran on, and felt as in a dream:
But dream it was not; no! – I fix'd my eyes

On the mid stream and saw the spirits rise;
I saw my father on the water stand,
And hold a thin pale boy in either hand;
And there they glided ghastly on the top
Of the salt flood, and never touch'd a drop:
I would have struck them, but they knew th' intent,
And smiled upon the oar, and down they went.
   'Now, from that day, whenever I began
To dip my net, there stood the hard old man –
He and those boys: I humbled me and pray'd
They would be gone; – they heeded not, but stay'd:
Nor could I turn, nor would the boat go by,
But gazing on the spirits, there was I:
They bade me leap to death, but I was loth to die:
And every day, as sure as day arose,
Would these three spirits meet me ere the close;
To hear and mark them daily was my doom,
And "Come," they said, with weak, sad voices, "come."
To row away with all my strength I try'd,
But there were they, hard by me in the tide,
The three unbodied forms – and "Come," still "come," they
   cried.
   'Fathers should pity – but this old man shook
His hoary locks, and froze me by a look:
Thrice, when I struck them, through the water came
A hollow groan, that weaken'd all my frame:
"Father!" said I, "have mercy:" – He replied,
I know not what – the angry spirit lied, –
"Didst thou not draw thy knife?" said he: – 'Twas true,
But I had pity and my arm withdrew:
He cried for mercy which I kindly gave,
But he has no compassion in his grave,
   'There were three places, where they ever rose, –
The whole long river has not such as those, –
Places accursed, where, if a man remain,

He'll see the things which strike him to the brain;
And there they made me on my paddle lean,
And look at them for hours; – accursed scene.
When they would glide to that smooth eddy-space,
Then bid me leap and join them in the place;
And at my groans each little villain sprite
Enjoy'd my pains and vanish'd in delight.

'In one fierce summer-day, when my poor brain
Was burning hot and cruel was my pain,
Then came this father-foe, and there he stood
With his two boys again upon the flood;
There was more mischief in their eyes, more glee
In their pale faces when they glared at me:
Still did they force me on the oar to rest,
And when they saw me fainting and oppress'd,
He, with his hand, the old man, scoop'd the flood,
And there came flame about him mix'd with blood;
He bade me stoop and look upon the place,
Then flung the hot-red liquor in my face;
Burning it blazed, and then I roar'd for pain,
I thought the demons would have turn'd my brain.

'Still there they stood, and forced me to behold
A place of horrors – they cannot be told –
Where the flood open'd, there I heard the shriek
Of tortured guilt – no earthly tongue can speak:
"All days alike! for ever!" did they say,
"And unremitted torments every day" –
Yes, so they said:' – But here he ceased and gazed
On all around, affrighten'd and amazed;
And still he tried to speak, and look'd in dread
Of frighten'd females gathering round his bed;
Then dropp'd exhausted and appear'd at rest,
Till the strong foe the vital powers possess'd:
Then with an inward, broken voice he cried,
'Again they come,' and mutter'd as he died.

Tales

from The Dumb Orators

As a male turkey straggling on the green,
When by fierce harriers, terriers, mongrels seen,
He feels the insult of the noisy train,
And skulks aside, though moved by much disdain;
But when that turkey, at his own barn-door,
Seen one poor straying puppy and no more,
(A foolish puppy who had left the pack,
Thoughtless what foe was threat'ning at his back,)
He moves about, as ship prepared to sail,
He hoists his proud rotundity of tail,
The half-seal'd eyes and changeful neck he shows,
Where, in its quick'ning colours, vengeance glows;
From red to blue the pendant wattles turn,
Blue mix'd with red, as matches when they burn;
And thus th' intruding snarler to oppose,
Urged by enkindling wrath, he gobbling goes.
So look'd our hero in his wrath, his cheeks
Flush'd with fresh fires and glow'd in tingling streaks;
His breath by passion's force awhile restrain'd;
Like a stopp'd current, greater force regain'd,
So spoke, so look'd he, every eye and ear
Were fix'd to view him, or were turn'd to hear.

from The Gentleman Farmer

Fix'd in his farm, he soon display'd his skill
In small-boned lambs, the horse-hoe, and the drill;
From these he rose to themes of nobler kind,
And show'd the riches of a fertile mind;
To all around their visits he repaid,
And thus his mansion and himself display'd,
His rooms were stately, rather fine than neat.
And guests politely call'd his house a seat;
At much expense was each apartment graced,
His taste was gorgeous, but it still was taste;
In full festoons the crimson curtains fell,
The sofas rose in bold elastic swell;
Mirrors in gilded frames display'd the tints
Of glowing carpets and of colour'd prints;
The weary eye saw every object shine,
And all was costly, fanciful, and fine.

from Procrastination

Month after month was pass'd, and all were spent
In quiet comfort and in rich content:
Miseries there were, and woes the world around,
But these had not her pleasant dwelling found;
She knew that mothers grieved, and widows wept,
And she was sorry, said her prayers, and slept:
Thus pass'd the seasons, and to Dinah's board
Gave what the seasons to the rich afford;
For she indulged, nor was her heart so small,
That one strong passion should engross it all.
A love of splendour now with av'rice strove,

And oft appear'd to be the stronger love:
A secret pleasure fill'd the widow's breast,
When she reflected on the hoards possess'd;
But livelier joy inspired th' ambitious maid,
When she the purchase of those hoards display'd:
In small but splendid room she loved to see
That all was placed in view and harmony;
There, as with eager glance she look'd around,
She much delight in every object found;
While books devout were near her – to destroy,
Should it arise, an overflow of joy.
  Within that fair apartment, guests might see
The comforts cull'd for wealth by vanity:
Around the room an Indian paper blazed,
With lively tint and figures boldly raised;
Silky and soft upon the floor below,
Th' elastic carpet rose with crimson glow;
All things around implied both cost and care,
What met the eye was elegant or rare:
Some curious trifles round the room were laid,
By hope presented to the wealthy maid:
Within a costly case of varnish'd wood,
In level rows, her polish'd volumes stood;
Shown as a favour to a chosen few,
To prove what beauty for a book could do:
A silver urn with curious work was fraught;
A silver lamp from Grecian pattern wrought:
Above her head, all gorgeous to behold,
A time-piece stood on feet of burnish'd gold;
A stag's head crest adorned the pictured case,
Through the pure crystal shone th' enamell'd face;
And while on brilliants moved the hands of steel,
It click'd from pray'r to pray'r, from meal to meal.

from The Patron

'Twas autumn yet, and many a day must frown
On Brandon-Hall, ere went my lord to town;
Meantime the father, who had heard his boy
Lived in a round of luxury and joy,
And justly thinking that the youth was one
Who, meeting danger, was unskill'd to shun;
Knowing his temper, virtue, spirit, zeal,
How prone to hope and trust, believe and feel;
These on the parent's soul their weight impress'd,
And thus he wrote the counsels of his breast.

'John, thou'rt a genius; thou hast some pretence,
I think, to wit, but hast thou sterling sense?
That which, like gold, may through the world go forth,
And always pass for what 'tis truly worth?
Whereas this genius, like a bill, must take
Only the value our opinions make.

'Men famed for wit, of dangerous talents vain,
Treat those of common parts with proud disdain;
The powers that wisdom would, improving, hide,
They blaze abroad with inconsid'rate pride;
While yet but mere probationers for fame,
They seize the honour they should then disclaim:
Honour so hurried to the light must fade,
The lasting laurels flourish in the shade.

'Genius is jealous; I have heard of some
Who, if unnoticed grew perversely dumb;
Nay, different talents would their envy raise;
Poets have sicken'd at a dancer's praise;
And one, the happiest writer of his time,
Grew pale at hearing Reynolds was sublime;
That Rutland's duchess wore a heavenly smile –
And I, said he, neglected all the while!

'A waspish tribe are these, on gilded wings,
Humming their lays, and brandishing their stings;
And thus they move their friends and foes among,
Prepared for soothing or satiric song.

'Hear me, my boy; thou hast a virtuous mind –
But be thy virtues of the sober kind;
Be not a Quixote, ever up in arms
To give the guilty and the great alarms:
If never heeded, thy attack is vain;
And if they heed thee, they'll attack again;
Then too in striking at that heedless rate,
Thou in an instant may'st decide thy fate.

'Leave admonition – let the vicar give
Rules how the nobles of his flock should live:
Nor take that simple fancy to thy brain,
That thou canst cure the wicked and the vain.

'Our Pope, they say, once entertain'd the whim,
Who fear'd not God should be afraid of him;
But grant they fear'd him, was it further said,
That he reform'd the hearts he made afraid?
Did Chartres mend? Ward, Waters, and a score
Of flagrant felons, with his floggings sore?
Was Cibber silenced? No: with vigour bless'd,
And brazen front, half earnest, half in jest,
He dared the bard to battle, and was seen
In all his glory match'd with Pope and spleen;
Himself he stripp'd, the harder blow to hit,
Then boldly match'd his ribaldry with wit;
The poet's conquest Truth and Time proclaim,
But yet the battle hurt his peace and fame.

'Strive not too much for favour; seem at ease,
And rather pleased thyself, than bent to please:
Upon thy lord with decent care attend,
But not too near; thou canst not be a friend;
And favourite be not, 'tis a dangerous post –

Is gain'd by labour, and by fortune lost:
Talents like thine may make a man approved,
But other talents trusted and beloved.
Look round, my son, and thou wilt early see
The kind of man thou art not form'd to be.
    'The real favourites of the great are they
Who to their views and wants attention pay,
And pay it ever; who, with all their skill,
Dive to the heart, and learn the secret will;
If that be vicious, soon can they provide
The favourite ill, and o'er the soul preside;
For vice is weakness, and the artful know
Their power increases as the passions grow;
If indolent the pupil, hard their task;
Such minds will ever for amusement ask:
And great the labour: for a man to choose
Objects for one whom nothing can amuse;
For ere those objects can the soul delight,
They must to joy the soul herself excite;
Therefore it is, this patient, watchful kind
With gentle friction stir the drowsy mind:
Fix'd on their end, with caution they proceed,
And sometimes give, and sometimes take the lead;
Will now a hint convey, and then retire,
And let the spark awake the lingering fire;
Or seek new joys and livelier pleasures bring,
To give the jaded sense a quick'ning spring.
    'These arts, indeed, my son must not pursue;
Nor must he quarrel with the tribe that do:
It is not safe another's crimes to know,
Nor is it wise our proper worth to show: –
"My lord," you say, "engaged me for that worth;" –
True, and preserve it ready to come forth:
If question'd, fairly answer – and that done,
Shrink back, be silent, and thy father's son;

For they who doubt thy talents scorn thy boast,
But they who grant them will dislike thee most:
Observe the prudent; they in silence sit,
Display no learning, and affect no wit;
They hazard nothing, nothing they assume,
But know the useful art of *acting dumb*.
Yet to their eyes each varying look appears,
And every word finds entrance at their ears.

from The Widow's Tale

To farmer Moss, in Langar Vale, came down
His only daughter, from her school in town;
A tender, timid maid! who knew not how
To pass a pig-sty, or to face a cow:
Smiling she came, with petty talents graced,
A fair complexion, and a slender waist.
   Used to spare meals, disposed in manner pure,
Her father's kitchen she could ill endure;
Where by the steaming beef he hungry sat,
And laid at once a pound upon his plate;
Hot from the field, her eager brother seized
An equal part, and hunger's rage appeased;
The air, surcharged with moisture, flagg'd around,
And the offended damsel sigh'd and frown'd;
The swelling fat in lumps conglomerate laid,
And fancy's sickness seized the loathing maid;
But when the men beside their station took,
The maidens with them, and with these the cook;
When one huge wooden bowl before them stood,
Fill'd with huge balls of farinaceous food;
With bacon, mass saline, where never lean
Beneath the brown and bristly rind was seen;
When from a single horn the party drew

Their copious draughts of heavy ale and new;
When the coarse cloth she saw, with many a stain,
Soil'd by rude hinds who cut and came again –
She could not breathe; but, with a heavy sigh,
Rein'd the fair neck, and shut th' offended eye;
She minced the sanguine flesh in frustums fine,
And wonder'd much to see the creatures dine:
When she resolved her father's heart to move,
If hearts of farmers were alive to love.

from The Lover's Journey

Again the country was enclosed, a wide
And sandy road has banks on either side;
Where, lo! a hollow on the left appear'd,
And there a gipsy-tribe their tent had rear'd;
'Twas open spread, to catch the morning sun,
And they had now their early meal begun,
When two brown boys just left their grassy seat,
The early trav'ller with their pray'rs to greet:
While yet Orlando held his pence in hand,
He saw their sister on her duty stand;
Some twelve years old, demure, affected, sly,
Prepared the force of early powers to try;
Sudden a look of languor he descries,
And well-feign'd apprehension in her eyes;
Train'd but yet savage, in her speaking face
He mark'd the features of her vagrant race;
When a light laugh and roguish leer express'd
The vice implanted in her youthful breast:
Forth from the tent her elder brother came,
Who seem'd offended, yet forbore to blame
The young designer, but could only trace

The looks of pity in the trav'ller's face:
Within, the father, who from fences nigh
Had brought the fuel for the fire's supply,
Watch'd now the feeble blaze, and stood dejected by:
On ragged rug, just borrow'd from the bed,
And by the hand of coarse indulgence fed,
In dirty patchwork negligently dress'd,
Reclined the wife, an infant at her breast;
In her wild face some touch of grace remain'd,
Of vigour palsied and of beauty stain'd;
Her blood-shot eyes on her unheeding mate
Were wrathful turn'd, and seem'd her wants to state,
Cursing his tardy aid – her mother there
With gipsy-state engross'd the only chair;
Solemn and dull her look; with such she stands,
And reads the milk-maid's fortune in her hands,
Tracing the lines of life; assumed through years,
Each feature now the steady falsehood wears;
With hard and savage eye she views the food,
And grudging pinches their intruding brood;
Last in the group, the worn-out grandsire sits
Neglected, lost, and living but by fits;
Useless, despised, his worthless labours done,
And half protected by the vicious son,
Who half supports him; he with heavy glance
Views the young ruffians who around him dance;
And, by the sadness in his face, appears
To trace the progress of their future years:
Through what strange course of misery, vice, deceit,
Must wildly wander each unpractised cheat!
What shame and grief, what punishment and pain,
Sport of fierce passions, must each child sustain –
Ere they like him approach their latter end,
Without a hope, a comfort, or a friend!

from The 'Squire and the Priest

The bells had toll'd – arrived the time of prayer,
The flock assembled, and the 'squire was there:
And now can poet sing, or proseman say,
The disappointment of that trying day?
   As he who long had train'd a favourite steed,
(Whose blood and bone gave promise of his speed,)
Sanguine with hope, he runs with partial eye
O'er every feature, and his bets are high;
Of triumph sure, he sees the rivals start,
And waits their coming with exulting heart;
Forestalling glory, with impatient glance,
And sure to see his conquering steed advance;
The conquering steed advances – luckless day!
A rival's Herod bears the prize away.
Nor second his, nor third, but lagging last,
With hanging head he comes, by all surpass'd:
Surprise and wrath the owner's mind inflame,
Love turns to scorn, and glory ends in shame; –
Thus waited, high in hope, the partial 'squire,
Eager to hear, impatient to admire:
When the young preacher in the tones that find
A certain passage to the kindling mind,
With air and accent strange, impressive, sad,
Alarm'd the judge – he trembled for the lad;
But when the text announced the power of grace,
Amazement scowl'd upon his clouded face,
At this degenerate son of his illustrious race;
Staring he stood, till hope again arose,
That James might well define the words he chose:
For this he listen'd – but alas! he found
The preacher always on forbidden ground.
   And now the uncle left the hated pew,

With James, and James's conduct in his view;
A long farewell to all his favourite schemes!
For now no crazed fanatic's frantic dreams
Seem'd vile as James's conduct, or as James:
All he had long derided, hated, fear'd,
This from the chosen youth the uncle heard; –
The needless pause, the fierce disorder'd air,
The groan for sin, the vehemence of prayer,
Gave birth to wrath, that, in a long discourse
Of grace, triumphant rose to four-fold force;
He found his thoughts despised, his rules transgress'd,
And while the anger kindled in his breast,
The pain must be endured that could not be express'd:
Each new idea more inflamed his ire,
As fuel thrown upon a rising fire:
A hearer yet, he sought by threatening sign
To ease his heart, and awe the young divine;
But James refused those angry looks to meet,
Till he dismiss'd his flock, and left his seat:
Exhausted then he felt his trembling frame,
But fix'd his soul – his sentiments the same;
And therefore wise it seem'd to fly from rage,
And seek for shelter in his parsonage:
There, if forsaken, yet consoled to find
Some comforts left, though not a few resign'd;
There, if he lost an erring parent's love,
An honest conscience must the cause approve;
If the nice palate were no longer fed,
The mind enjoy'd delicious thoughts instead;
And if some part of earthly good was flown,
Still was the tithe of ten good farms his own.

from Resentment

A dreadful winter came, each day severe,
Misty when mild, and icy cold when clear;
And still the humble dealer took his load,
Returning slow, and shivering on the road:
The lady still relentless, saw him come,
And said – 'I wonder, has the wretch a home?'
'A hut! a hovel!' – 'Then his fate appears
To suit his crime:' – 'Yes lady, not his years; –
No! nor his sufferings – nor that form decay'd.'
'Well, let the parish give its paupers aid:
You must the vileness of his acts allow;'
'And you, dear lady, that he feels it now.'
'When such dissemblers on their deeds reflect,
Can they the pity they refused expect?
He that doth evil, evil shall he dread.' –
'The snow,' quoth Susan, 'falls upon his bed –
It blows beside the thatch – it melts upon his head' –
''Tis weakness, child, for grieving guilt to feel:'
'Yes, but he never sees a wholesome meal;
Through his bare dress appears his shrivell'd skin,
And ill he fares without, and worse within:
With that weak body, lame, diseased, and slow,
What cold, pain, peril, must the sufferer know!'
'Think on his crime.' – 'Yes, sure 'twas very wrong;
But look, (God bless him!) how he gropes along.' –
'Brought me to shame.' – 'Oh! yes, I know it all –
What cutting blast! and he can scarcely crawl;
He freezes as he moves – he dies! if he should fall:
With cruel fierceness drives this icy sleet –
And must a Christian perish in the street,
In sight of Christians? – There! at last, he lies; –
Nor unsupported can he ever rise;

He cannot live.' – 'But is he fit to die?' –
Here, Susan softly mutter'd a reply,
Look'd round the room – said something of its state,
Dives the rich, and Lazarus at his gate;
And then aloud – 'In pity do behold
The man affrighten'd, weeping, trembling, cold:
Oh! how those flakes of snow their entrance win
Through the poor rags, and keep the frost within;
His very heart seems frozen as he goes,
Leading that starved companion of his woes:
He tried to pray – his lips, I saw them move,
And he so turn'd his piteous looks above;
But the fierce wind the willing heart opposed,
And, ere he spoke, the lips in misery closed:
Poor suffering object! yes, for ease you pray'd,
And God will hear – he only, I'm afraid.'
    'Peace! Susan, peace! Pain ever follows sin.' –
'Ah! then,' thought Susan, 'when will ours begin?
'When reach'd his home, to what a cheerless fire
And chilling bed will those cold limbs retire!
Yet ragged, wretched as it is, that bed
Takes half the space of his contracted shed;
I saw the thorns beside the narrow grate,
With straw collected in a putrid state:
There will he, kneeling, strive the fire to raise,
And that will warm him, rather than the blaze;
The sullen, smoky blaze, that cannot last
One moment after his attempt is past:
And I so warmly and so purely laid,
To sink to rest – indeed, I am afraid.' –
'Know you his conduct?' – 'Yes, indeed, I know –
And how he wanders in the wind and snow:
Safe in our rooms the threat'ning storm we hear,
But he feels strongly what we faintly fear.'
'Wilful was rich, and he the storm defied;

Wilful is poor, and must the storm abide;'
Said the stern lady – ''Tis in vain to feel;
Go and prepare the chicken for our meal.'

   Susan her task reluctantly began,
And utter'd as she went – 'The poor old man!' –
But while her soft and ever-yielding heart
Made strong protest against her lady's part,
The lady's self began to think it wrong,
To feel so wrathful and resent so long.

   'No more the wretch would she receive again,
No more behold him – but she would sustain;
Great his offence, and evil was his mind –
But he had suffer'd, and she would be kind:
She spurn'd such baseness, and she found within
A fair acquittal from so foul a sin;
Yet she too err'd, and must of Heaven expect
To be rejected, him should she reject.'

   Susan was summon'd – 'I'm about to do
A foolish act, in part seduced by you;
Go to the creature – say that I intend,
Foe to his sins, to be his sorrow's friend;
Take, for his present comforts, food and wine,
And mark his feelings at this act of mine:
Observe if shame be o'er his features spread,
By his own victim to be soothed and fed;
But, this inform him, that it is not love
That prompts my heart, that duties only move:
Say, that no merits in his favour plead,
But miseries only, and his abject need;
Nor bring me grov'ling thanks, nor high-flown praise;
I would his spirits, not his fancy raise:
Give him no hope that I shall ever more
A man so vile to my esteem restore;
But warn him rather, that, in time of rest,
His crimes be all remember'd and confess'd:

I know not all that form the sinner's debt,
But there is one that he must not forget.'
   The mind of Susan prompted her with speed
To act her part in every courteous deed:
All that was kind she was prepared to say,
And keep the lecture for a future day;
When he had all life's comforts by his side,
Pity might sleep, and good advice be tried.
   This done, the mistress felt disposed to look,
As self-approving, on a pious book:
Yet, to her native bias still inclined,
She felt her act too merciful and kind;
But when, long musing on the chilling scene
So lately past – the frost and sleet so keen –
The man's whole misery in a single view –
Yes! she could think some pity was his due.
   Thus fix'd, she heard not her attendant glide
With soft slow step – till, standing by her side,
The trembling servant gasp'd for breath, and shed
Relieving tears, then utter'd – 'He is dead!'
   'Dead!' said the startled lady; 'Yes, he fell
Close at the door where he was wont to dwell;
There his sole friend, the ass, was standing by,
Half dead himself, to see his master die.'
   'Expired he then, good Heaven! for want of food?'
'No! crusts and water in a corner stood: –
To have this plenty, and to wait so long,
And to be right too late, is doubly wrong:
Then, every day to see him totter by,
And to forbear – Oh! what a heart had I!'
   'Blame me not, child; I tremble at the news.'
''Tis my own heart,' said Susan, 'I accuse:
To have this money in my purse – to know
What grief was his, and what to grief we owe;
To see him often, always to conceive

How he must pine and languish, groan and grieve;
And every day in ease and peace to dine,
And rest in comfort! – what a heart is mine!' –

from The Wager

Clubb, with these notions, cast his eye around,
And one so easy soon a partner found.
The lady chosen was of good repute;
Meekness she had not, and was seldom mute;
Though quick to anger, still she loved to smile;
And would be calm if men would wait awhile:
She knew her duty, and she loved her way,
More pleased in truth to govern than obey:
She heard her priest with reverence, and her spouse
As one who felt the pressure of her vows:
Useful and civil, all her friends confess'd –
Give her her way, and she would choose the best;
Though some indeed a sly remark would make –
Give it her not, and she would choose to take.
All this, when Clubb some cheerful months had spent,
He saw, confess'd, and said he was content.
Counter meantime selected, doubted, weigh'd,
And then brought home a young complying maid; –
A tender creature, full of fears as charms,
A beauteous nursling from its mother's arms;
A soft, sweet blossom, such as men must love,
But to preserve must keep it in the stove:
She had a mild, subdued, expiring look –
Raise but the voice, and this fair creature shook;
Leave her alone, she felt a thousand fears –
Chide, and she melted into floods of tears;
Fondly she pleaded and would gently sigh,

For very pity, or she knew not why;
One whom to govern none could be afraid –
Hold up the finger, this meek thing obey'd;
Her happy husband had the easiest task –
Say but his will, no question would she ask;
She sought no reasons, no affairs she knew,
Of business spoke not, and had nought to do.

from The Convert

  With spirit high John learn'd the world to brave,
And in both senses was a ready knave;
Knave as of old, obedient, keen, and quick,
Knave as at present, skill'd to shift and trick;
Some humble part of many trades he caught,
He for the builder and the painter wrought;
For serving-maids on secret errands ran,
The waiter's helper, and the hostler's man;
And when he chanced (oft chanced he) place to lose,
His varying genius shone in blacking shoes:
A midnight fisher by the pond he stood,
Assistant poacher, he o'erlook'd the wood;
At an election John's impartial mind
Was to no cause nor candidate confined;
To all in turn he full allegiance swore,
And in his hat the various badges bore:
His liberal soul with every sect agreed,
Unheard their reasons, he received their creed;
At church he deign'd the organ-pipes to fill,
And at the meeting sang both loud and shrill:
But the full purse these different merits gain'd,
By strong demands his lively passions drain'd;
Liquors he loved of each inflaming kind,

To midnight revels flew with ardent mind;
Too warm at cards, a losing game he play'd,
To fleecing beauty his attention paid;
His boiling passions were by oaths express'd,
And lies he made his profit and his jest.
   Such was the boy, and such the man had been,
But fate or happier fortune changed the scene;
A fever seized him, 'He should surely die –'
He fear'd, and lo! a friend was praying by;
With terror moved, this teacher he address'd,
And all the errors of his youth confess'd:
The good man kindly cleared the sinner's way
To lively hope, and counsell'd him to pray;
Who then resolved, should he from sickness rise,
To quit cards, liquors, poaching, oaths, and lies:
His health restored, he yet resolved, and grew
True to his masters, to their meeting true;
His old companions at his sober face
Laugh'd loud, while he, attesting it was grace,
With tears besought them all his calling to embrace:
To his new friends such convert gave applause,
Life to their zeal, and glory to their cause:
Though terror wrought the mighty change, yet strong
Was the impression, and it lasted long;
John at the lectures due attendance paid,
A convert meek, obedient, and afraid.
His manners strict, though form'd on fear alone,
Pleased the grave friends, nor less his solemn tone,
The lengthen'd face of care, the low and inward groan:
The stern good men exulted, when they saw
Those timid looks of penitence and awe;
Nor thought that one so passive, humble, meek,
Had yet a creed and principles to seek.
The faith that reason finds, confirms, avows,
The hopes, the views, the comforts he allows –

These were not his, who by his feelings found,
And by them only, that his faith was sound;
Feelings of terror these, for evil past,
Feelings of hope, to be received at last;
Now weak, now lively, changing with the day,
These were his feelings, and he felt his way.

   Sprung from such sources, will this faith remain
While these supporters can their strength retain:
As heaviest weights the deepest rivers pass,
While icy chains fast bind the solid mass;
So, born of feelings, faith remains secure,
Long as their firmness and their strength endure:
But when the waters in their channel glide,
A bridge must bear us o'er the threat'ning tide;
Such bridge is reason, and there faith relies,
Whether the varying spirits fall or rise.

from The Brothers

   Ill were the tidings that arrived from sea,
The worthy George must now a cripple be;
His leg was lopp'd; and though his heart was sound,
Though his brave captain was with glory crown'd –
Yet much it vex'd him to repose on shore,
An idle log, and be of use no more:
True, he was sure that Isaac would receive
All of his brother that the foe might leave;
To whom the seaman his design had sent,
Ere from the port the wounded hero went:
His wealth and expectations told, he 'knew
Wherein they fail'd, what Isaac's love would do;
That he the grog and cabin would supply,
Where George at anchor during life would lie.'

The landman read – and, reading, grew distress'd: –
'Could he resolve t' admit so poor a guest?
Better at Greenwich might the sailor stay,
Unless his purse could for his comforts pay;'
So Isaac judged, and to his wife appeal'd,
But yet acknowledged it was best to yield:
'Perhaps his pension, with what sums remain
Due or unsquander'd, may the man maintain;
Refuse we must not.' – With a heavy sigh
The lady heard, and made her kind reply: –
'Nor would I wish it, Isaac, were we sure
How long his crazy building will endure;
Like an old house, that every day appears
About to fall – he may be propp'd for years;
For a few months, indeed, we might comply,
But these old batter'd fellows never die.'

from The Learned Boy

The love of order – I the thing receive
From reverend men, and I in part believe –
Shows a clear mind and clean, and whoso needs
This love, but seldom in the world succeeds;
And yet with this some other love must be,
Ere I can fully to the fact agree:
Valour and study may by order gain,
By order sovereigns hold more steady reign;
Through all the tribes of nature order runs,
And rules around in systems and in suns:
Still has the love of order found a place,
With all that's low, degrading, mean, and base,
With all that merits scorn, and all that meets disgrace:
In the cold miser, of all change afraid,

In pompous men in public seats obey'd:
In humble placement, heralds, solemn drones,
Fanciers of flowers, and lads like Stephen Jones;
Order to these is armour and defence,
And love of method serves in lack of sense.

Tales of the Hall

from The Hall

George loved the cause of freedom, but reproved
All who with wild and boyish ardour loved;
Those who believed they never could be free,
Except when fighting for their liberty;
Who by their very clamour and complaint
Invite coercion or enforce restraint:
He thought a trust so great, so good a cause,
Was only to be kept by guarding laws;
For public blessings firmly to secure,
We must a lessening of the good endure.
The public waters are to none denied,
All drink the stream, but only few must guide;
There must be reservoirs to hold supply,
And channels form'd to send the blessing by;
The public good must be a private care,
None all they would may have, but all a share:
So we must freedom with restraint enjoy,
What crowds possess they will, uncheck'd, destroy;
And hence, that freedom may to all be dealt,
Guards must be fix'd, and safety must be felt.
So thought our squire, nor wish'd the guards t' appear
So strong, that safety might be bought too dear;
The constitution was the ark that he
Join'd to support with zeal and sanctity,
Nor would expose it, as th' accursed son
His father's weakness, to be gazed upon.
I for that freedom make, said he, my prayer,
That suits with all, like atmospheric air;
That is to mortal man by heaven assign'd,

Who cannot bear a pure and perfect kind:
The lighter gas, that taken in the frame,
The spirit heats, and sets the blood in flame,
Such is the freedom which when men approve,
They know not what a dangerous thing they love.

*

Through ways more rough had fortune RICHARD led,
The world he traversed was the book he read;
Hence clashing notions and opinions strange
Lodged in his mind; all liable to change.
  By nature generous, open, daring, free,
The vice he hated was hypocrisy:
Religious notions, in her latter years,
His mother gave, admonish'd by her fears;
To these he added, as he chanced to read
A pious work or learn a christian creed:
He heard the preacher by the highway side,
The church's teacher, and the meeting's guide;
And mixing all their matters in his brain,
Distill'd a something he could ill explain;
But still it served him for his daily use,
And kept his lively passions from abuse;
For he believed, and held in reverence high,
The truth so dear to man – 'not all shall die.'
The minor portions of his creed hung loose,
For time to shapen and an whole produce;
This love effected and a favourite maid,
With clearer views, his honest flame repaid;
Hers was the thought correct, the hope sublime,
She shaped his creed, and did the work of time.

from The Brothers

   Ease leads to habit, as success to ease,
He lives by rule who lives himself to please,
For change is trouble, and a man of wealth
Consults his quiet as he guards his health;
And habit now on George had sovereign power,
His actions all had their accustom'd hour:
At the fix'd time he slept, he walk'd, he read,
Or sought his grounds, his gruel, and his bed;
For every season he with caution dress'd,
And morn and eve had the appropriate vest;
He talk'd of early mists, and night's cold air,
And in one spot was fix'd his worship's chair.
   But not a custom yet on Richard's mind
Had force, or him to certain modes confined;
To him no joy such frequent visits paid,
That habit by its beaten track was made:
He was not one who at his ease could say,
'We'll live to-morrow as we lived to-day;'
But he and his were as the ravens fed,
As the day came it brought the daily bread.

*

   Now squire and rector were return'd to school,
And spoke of him who there had sovereign rule:
He was, it seem'd, a tyrant of the sort
Who make the cries of tortured boys his sport;
One of a race, if not extinguish'd, tamed,
The flogger now is of the act ashamed;
But this great mind all mercy's calls withstood,
This Holofernes was a man of blood.
   'Students,' he said, 'like horses on the road,
Must well be lash'd before they take the load;

They may be willing for a time to run,
But you must whip them ere the work be done:
To tell a boy, that, if he will improve,
His friends will praise him, and his parents love,
Is doing nothing – he has not a doubt
But they will love him, nay, applaud, without:
Let no fond sire a boy's ambition trust,
To make him study, let him see he must.'

    Such his opinion; and to prove it true,
At least sincere, it was his practice too:
Pluto they call'd him, and they named him well,
'Twas not an heaven where he was pleased to dwell:
From him a smile was like the Greenland sun,
Surprising, nay portentous, when it shone;
Or like the lightning, for the sudden flash
Prepared the children for the thunder's crash.

    O! had Narcissa, when she fondly kiss'd
The weeping boy whom she to school dismiss'd,
Had she beheld him shrinking from the arm
Uplifted high to do the greater harm,
Then seen her darling stript, and that pure white,
And – O! her soul had fainted at the sight;
And with those looks that love could not withstand,
She would have cried, 'Barbarian, hold thy hand!'
In vain! no grief to this stern soul could speak,
No iron-tear roll down this Pluto's cheek.

    Thus far they went, half earnest, half in jest,
Then turn'd to themes of deeper interest;
While Richard's mind, that for awhile had stray'd,
Call'd home its powers, and due attention paid.

from Adventures of Richard

It was a fair and mild autumnal sky,
And earth's ripe treasures met th' admiring eye,
As a rich beauty, when her bloom is lost,
Appears with more magnificence and cost:
The wet and heavy grass, where feet had stray'd,
Not yet erect, the wanderer's way betray'd;
Showers of the night had swell'd the deep'ning rill,
The morning breeze had urged the quick'ning mill;
Assembled rooks had wing'd their sea-ward flight,
By the same passage to return at night,
While proudly o'er them hung the steady kite,
Then turn'd him back, and left the noisy throng,
Nor deign'd to know them as he sail'd along.
Long yellow leaves, from oziers, strew'd around,
Choked the small stream, and hush'd the feeble sound;
While the dead foliage dropt from loftier trees
Our squire beheld not with his wonted ease,
But to his own reflections made reply,
And said aloud, 'Yes! doubtless we must die.'

'We must;' said Richard, 'and we would not live
To feel what dotage and decay will give;
But we yet taste whatever we behold,
The morn is lovely, though the air is cold:
There is delicious quiet in this scene,
At once so rich, so varied, so serene;
Sounds too delight us, – each discordant tone
Thus mingled please, that fail to please alone;
This hollow wind, this rustling of the brook,
The farm-yard noise, the woodman at yon oak –
See, the axe falls! – now listen to the stroke!
That gun itself, that murders all this peace,
Adds to the charm, because it soon must cease.'

*

'To me the wives of seamen loved to tell
What storms endanger'd men esteem'd so well;
What wond'rous things in foreign parts they saw,
Lands without bounds, and people without law.
    'No ships were wreck'd upon that fatal beach,
But I could give the luckless tale of each;
Eager I look'd, till I beheld a face
Of one disposed to paint their dismal case;
Who gave the sad survivors' doleful tale,
From the first brushing of the mighty gale
Until they struck; and, suffering in their fate,
I long'd the more they should its horrors state;
While some, the fond of pity, would enjoy
The earnest sorrows of the feeling boy.
I sought the men return'd from regions cold,
The frozen straits, where icy mountains roll'd;
Some I could win to tell me serious tales
Of boats uplifted by enormous whales,
Or, when harpoon'd, how swiftly through the sea
The wounded monsters with the cordage flee,
Yet some uneasy thoughts assail'd me then,
The monsters warr'd not with, nor wounded men:
The smaller fry we take, with scales and fins,
Who gasp and die – this adds not to our sins;
But so much blood! warm life, and frames so large
To strike to murder – seem'd an heavy charge.
    'They told of days, where many goes to one –
Such days as ours; and how a larger sun,
Red, but not flaming, roll'd, with motion slow,
On the world's edge, and never dropt below.
    'There were fond girls, who took me to their side
To tell the story how their lovers died;
They praised my tender heart, and bade me prove
Both kind and constant when I came to love.
In fact, I lived for many an idle year

In fond pursuit of agitations dear;
For ever seeking, ever pleased to find,
The food I loved, I thought not of its kind;
It gave affliction while it brought delight,
And joy and anguish could at once excite.
   'One gusty day, now stormy and now still,
I stood apart upon the western hill,
And saw a race at sea: a gun was heard,
And two contending boats in sail appear'd:
Equal awhile; then one was left behind,
And for a moment had her chance resign'd,
When, in that moment, up a sail they drew –
Not used before – their rivals to pursue.
Strong was the gale! in hurry now there came
Men from the town, their thoughts, their fears the same;
And women too! affrighted maids and wives,
All deeply feeling for their sailor's lives.
   'The strife continued; in a glass we saw
The desperate efforts, and we stood in awe,
When the last boat shot suddenly before,
Then fill'd, and sank – and could be seen no more!
   'Then were those piercing shrieks, that frantic flight,
All hurried! all in tumult and affright!
A gathering crowd from different streets drew near,
All ask, all answer – none attend, none hear!
   'One boat is safe; and see! she backs her sail
To save the sinking – Will her care avail?
   'O! how impatient on the sands we tread,
And the winds roaring, and the women led,
As up and down they pace with frantic air,
And scorn a comforter, and will despair;
They know not who in either boat is gone,
But think the father, husband, lover, one.
   'And who is she apart? She dares not come
To join the crowd, yet cannot rest at home:

With what strong interest looks she at the waves,
Meeting and clashing o'er the seamen's graves:
'Tis a poor girl betroth'd – a few hours more,
And *he* will lie a corpse upon the shore.

from Ruth

   ' "Ah! my dear lad, I talk to you as one
Who knew the misery of an heart undone;
You know it not; but, dearest boy, when man,
Do not an ill because you find you can:
Where is the triumph? when such things men seek
They only drive to wickedness the weak.
   ' "Weak was poor Ruth, and this good man so hard,
That to her weakness he had no regard:
But we had two days' peace; he came, and then
My daughter whisper'd, 'Would there were no men!
None to admire or scorn us, none to vex
A simple, trusting, fond, believing sex;
Who truly love the worth that men profess,
And think too kindly for their happiness.' "
   'Poor Ruth! few heroines in the tragic page
Felt more than thee in thy contracted stage:
Fair, fond, and virtuous, they our pity move,
Impell'd by duty, agonized by love;
But no Mandane, who in dread has knelt
On the bare boards, has greater terrors felt
Nor been by warring passions more subdued
Than thou, by this man's grovelling wish pursued;
Doom'd to a parent's judgment, all unjust,
Doom'd the chance mercy of the world to trust,
Or to wed grossness and conceal disgust.
   ' "If Ruth was frail, she had a mind too nice

To wed with that which she beheld as vice;
To take a reptile, who, beneath a show
Of peevish zeal, let carnal wishes grow;
Proud and yet mean, forbidding and yet full
Of eager appetites, devout and dull,
Waiting a legal right that he might seize
His own, and his impatient spirit ease,
Who would at once his pride and love indulge,
His temper humour, and his spite divulge.

from Adventures of Richard Concluded

'The Vicar's self, still further to describe,
Was of a simple, but a studious tribe;
He from the world was distant, not retired,
Nor of it much possess'd, nor much desired:
Grave in his purpose, cheerful in his eye,
And with a look of frank benignity.
He lost his wife when they together past
Years of calm love, that triumph'd to the last.
He much of nature, not of man had seen,
Yet his remarks were often shrewd and keen;
Taught not by books t' approve or to condemn,
He gain'd but little that he knew from them;
He read with reverence and respect the few,
Whence he his rules and consolations drew;
But men and beasts, and all that lived or moved,
Were books to him; he studied them and loved.
    'He knew the plants in mountain, wood, or mead;
He knew the worms that on the foliage feed;
Knew the small tribes that 'scape the careless eye,
The plant's disease that breeds the embryo-fly;
And the small creatures who on bark or bough

Enjoy their changes, changed we know not how;
But now th' imperfect being scarcely moves,
And now takes wing and seeks the sky it loves.

from The Elder Brother

'My thrifty uncle, now return'd began
To stir within me what remained of man;
My powerful frenzy painted to the life,
And ask'd me if I took a dream to wife?
Debate ensued, and though not well content,
Upon a visit to his house I went:
He, the most saving of mankind, had still
Some kindred feeling; he would guide my will,
And teach me wisdom – so affection wrought,
That he to save me from destruction sought:
To him destruction, the most awful curse
Of misery's children, was – an empty purse!
He his own books approved, and thought the pen
An useful instrument for trading men;
But judged a quill was never to be slit
Except to make it for a merchant fit:
He, when informed how men of taste could write,
Look'd on his ledger with supreme delight;
Then would he laugh, and, with insulting joy,
Tell me aloud, 'that's poetry, my boy;
These are your golden numbers – them repeat,
The more you have, the more you'll find them sweet –
Their numbers move all hearts – no matter for their feet.
Sir, when a man composes in this style,
What is to him a critic's frown or smile?
What is the puppy's censure or applause
To the good man who on his banker draws,

Buys an estate, and writes upon the grounds,
'Pay to A. B. an hundred thousand pounds?'
Thus, my dear nephew, thus your talents prove;
Leave verse to poets, and the poor to love.'

*

'Twas in that chamber, Richard, I began
To think more deeply of the end of man:
Was it to jostle all his fellows by,
To run before them, and say, "here am I,
Fall down and worship?" – Was it, life throughout,
With circumspection keen to hunt about
As spaniels for their game, where might be found
Abundance more for coffers that abound?
Or was it life's enjoyments to prefer,
Like this poor girl, and then to die like her?
No! He, who gave the faculties, design'd
Another use for the immortal mind:
There is a state in which it will appear
With all the good and ill contracted here;
With gain and loss, improvement and defect;
And then, my soul! what hast thou to expect
For talents laid aside, life's waste, and time's neglect?
'Still as I went came other change – the frame
And features wasted, and yet slowly came
The end; and so inaudible the breath,
And still the breathing, we exclaim'd – 'tis death!
But death it was not: when, indeed, she died,
I sat and his last gentle stroke espied:
When – as it came – or did my fancy trace
That lively, lovely flushing o'er the face?
Bringing back all that my young heart impress'd!
It came – and went! – She sigh'd, and was at rest!

from The Sisters

'"Let me not have this gloomy view,
    About my room, around my bed;
But morning roses, wet with dew,
    To cool my burning brows instead.
As flowers that once in Eden grew,
    Let them their fragrant spirits shed,
And every day the sweets renew,
    Till I, a fading flower, am dead

'"Oh! let the herbs I loved to rear
    Give to my sense their perfumed breath;
Let them be placed about my bier,
    And grace the gloomy house of death.
I'll have my grave beneath an hill,
    Where, only Lucy's self shall know;
Where runs the pure pellucid rill
    Upon its gravelly bed below;
There violets on the borders blow,
    And insects their soft light display,
Till, as the morning sun-beams glow,
    The cold phosphoric fires decay.

'"That is the grave to Lucy shown,
    The soil a pure and silver sand,
The green cold moss above it grown,
    Unpluck'd of all but maiden hand:
In virgin earth, till then unturn'd,
    There let my maiden form be laid,
Nor let my changed clay be spurned,
    Nor for new guest that bed be made.

'"There will the lark, – the lamb, in sport,
  In air, – on earth, – securely play,
And Lucy to my grave resort,
  As innocent, but not so gay.
I will not have the churchyard ground,
  With bones all black and ugly brown,
To press my shivering body round,
  Or on my wasted limbs be thrown.

'"With ribs and skulls I will not sleep,
  In clammy beds of cold blue clay,
Through which the ringed earth-worms creep,
  And on the shrouded bosom prey;
I will not have the bell proclaim
  When those sad marriage rites begin,
And boys, without regard or shame,
  Press the vile mouldering masses in.

'"Say not, it is beneath my care;
  I cannot these cold truths allow;
These thoughts may not afflict me there,
  But, O! they vex and tease me now.
Raise not a turf, nor set a stone,
  That man a maiden's grave may trace,
But thou, my Lucy, come alone,
  And let affection find the place.

'"O! take me from a world I hate,
  Men cruel, selfish, sensual, cold;
And in some pure and blessed state
  Let me my sister minds behold:
From gross and sordid views refined
  Our heaven of spotless love to share
For only generous souls design'd
  And not a man to meet us there."'

from The Preceptor Husband

'They soon were wedded, and the nymph appear'd
By all her promised excellence endear'd:
Her words were kind, were cautious, and were few,
And she was proud – of what her husband knew.
   'Weeks pass'd away, some five or six, before,
Bless'd in the present, Finch could think of more:
A month was next upon a journey spent,
When to the lakes the fond companions went;
Then the gay town received them, and, at last,
Home to their mansion, man and wife, they pass'd.
   'And now in quiet way they came to live
On what their fortune, love, and hopes would give:
The honied moon had naught but silver rays,
And shone benignly on their early days;
The second moon a light less vivid shed,
And now the silver rays were tinged with lead.
They now began to look beyond the Hall,
And think what friends would make a morning-call;
Their former appetites return'd, and now
Both could their wishes and their tastes avow;
'Twas now no longer "just what you approve,"
But, "let the wild fowl be to-day, my love."
In fact the senses, drawn aside by force
Of a strong passion, sought their usual course.
   'Now to her music would the wife repair,
To which he listen'd once with eager air;
When there was so much harmony within,
That any note was sure its way to win;
But now the sweet melodious tones were sent
From the struck chords, and none cared where they went.
Full well we know that many a favourite air,
That charms a party, fails to charm a pair;

And as Augusta play'd she look'd around,
To see if one was dying at the sound:
But all were gone – a husband, wrapt in gloom,
Stalk'd careless, listless, up and down the room.

from The Old Bachelor

'Six years had past, and forty ere the six,
When Time began to play his usual tricks:
The locks once comely in a virgin's sight,
Locks of pure brown, display'd th' encroaching white;
And blood once fervid now to cool began,
And Time's strong pressure to subdue the man:
I rode or walk'd as I was wont before,
But now the bounding spirit was no more;
A moderate pace would now my body heat,
A walk of moderate length distress my feet.
I show'd my stranger-guest those hills sublime,
But said, "the view is poor, we need not climb."
At a friend's mansion I began to dread
The cold neat parlour, and the gay glazed bed;
At home I felt a more decided taste,
And must have all things in my order placed;
I ceased to hunt, my horses pleased me less,
My dinner more; I learn'd to play at chess;
I took my dog and gun, but saw the brute
Was disappointed that I did not shoot;
My morning walks I now could bear to lose,
And bless'd the shower that gave me not to choose:
In fact, I felt a languor stealing on;
The active arm, the agile hand were gone;
Small daily actions into habits grew,
And new dislike to forms and fashion new;

I loved my trees in order to dispose,
I numbor'd peaches, look'd how stocks arose,
Told the same story oft – in short, began to prose.

*

'I now was sixty, but could walk and eat:
My food was pleasant, and my slumbers sweet;
But what could urge me at a day so late
To think of women? – my unlucky fate.
'It was not sudden; I had no alarms,
But was attack'd when resting on my arms;
Like the poor soldier; when the battle raged
The man escaped, though twice or thrice engaged,
But when it ended, in a quiet spot
He fell, the victim of a random-shot.
'With my good friend the vicar oft I spent
The evening hours in quiet, as I meant;
He was a friend in whom, although untried
By ought severe, I found I could confide;
A pleasant, sturdy disputant was he,
Who had a daughter – such the Fates decree,
To prove how weak is man – poor yielding man, like me.
'Time after time the maid went out and in,
Ere love was yet beginning to begin;
The first awakening proof, the early doubt,
Rose from observing she went in and out.
My friend, though careless, seem'd my mind to explore,
"Why do you look so often at the door?"
I then was cautious, but it did no good,
For she, at least, my meanings understood;
But to the vicar nothing she convey'd
Of what she thought – she did not feel afraid.
'I must confess, this creature in her mind
Nor face had beauty that a man would blind;
No poet of her matchless charms would write,

Yet sober praise they fairly would excite:
She was a creature form'd man's heart to make
Serenely happy, not to pierce and shake;
If she were tried for breaking human hearts
Men would acquit her – she had not the arts;
Yet without art, at first without design,
She soon became the arbitress of mine;
Without pretensions – nay, without pretence,
But by a native strange intelligence
Women possess when they behold a man
Whom they can tease, and are assured they can;
Then 'tis their soul's delight and pride to reign
O'er the fond slave, to give him ease or pain,
And stretch and loose by turns the weighty viewless chain.
    'Though much she knew, yet nothing could she prove;
I had not yet confess'd the crime of love;
But in an hour when guardian-angels sleep,
I fail'd the secret of my soul to keep;
And then I saw the triumph in those eyes
That spoke – "Ay, now you are indeed my prize."
I almost thought I saw compassion, too,
For all the cruel things she meant to do.
Well I can call to mind the managed air
That gave no comfort, that brought no despair,
That in a dubious balance held the mind,
To each side turning, never much inclined.
    'She spoke with kindness – thought the honour high,
And knew not how to give a fit reply;
She could not, would not, dared not, must not deem
Such language proof of ought but my esteem;
It made her proud – she never could forget
My partial thoughts, – she felt her much in debt:
She who had never in her life indulged
The thought of hearing what I now divulged,
I who had seen so many and so much, –

It was an honour – she would deem it such:
Our different years, indeed, would put an end
To other views, but still her father's friend
To her, she humbly hoped, would his regard extend.
Thus saying nothing, all she meant to say,
She play'd the part the sex delights to play;
Now by some act of kindness giving scope
To the new workings of excited hope,
Then by an air of something like disdain,
But scarcely seen, repelling it again;
Then for a season, neither cold nor kind,
She kept a sort of balance in the mind,
And as his pole a dancer on the rope,
The equal poise on both sides kept me up.
     'Is it not strange that man can fairly view
Pursuit like this, and yet his point pursue?
While he the folly fairly will confess,
And even feel the danger of success?
But so it is, and nought the Circes care
How ill their victims with their poison fare,
When thus they trifle, and with quiet soul
Mix their ingredients in the maddening bowl.
Their high regard, the softness of their air,
The pitying grief that saddens at a prayer,
Their grave petitions for the peace of mind
That they determine you shall never find,
And all their vain amazement that a man
Like you should love – they wonder how you can.

from The Maid's Story

     'My father dying, to my mother left
An infant charge, of all things else bereft;

Poor, but experienced in the world, she knew
What others did, and judged what she could do;
Beauty she justly weigh'd, was never blind
To her own interest, and she read mankind:
She view'd my person with approving glance,
And judged the way my fortune to advance;
Taught me betimes that person to improve,
And make a lawful merchandize of love;
Bade me my temper in subjection keep,
And not permit my vigilance to sleep;
I was not one, a miss, who might presume
Now to be crazed by mirth, now sunk in gloom;
Nor to be fretful, vapourish, or give way
To spleen and anger, as the wealthy may;
But I must please, and all I felt of pride,
Contempt, and hatred, I must cast aside.

"Have not one friend," my mother cried, "not one;
That bane of our romantic triflers shun;
Suppose her true, can she afford you aid?
Suppose her false, your purpose is betray'd;
And then in dubious points, and matters nice,
How can you profit by a child's advice?
While you are writing on from post to post,
Your hour is over, and a man is lost;
Girls of their hearts are scribbling; their desires,
And what the folly of the heart requires,
Dupes to their dreams – but I the truth impart,
You cannot, child, afford to have a heart;
Think nothing of it; to yourself be true,
And keep life's first great business in your view; –
Take it, dear Martha, for a useful rule,
She who is poor is ugly or a fool;
Or, worse than either, has a bosom fill'd
With soft emotions, and with raptures thrill'd.

'"Read not too much, nor write in verse or prose,

For then you make the dull and foolish foes;
Yet those who do, deride not nor condemn,
It is not safe to raise up foes in them;
For though they harm you not, as blockheads do,
There is some malice in the scribbling crew."'

'Such her advice; full hard with her had dealt
The world, and she the usage keenly felt.

'"Keep your good name," she said, "and that to keep
You must not suffer vigilance to sleep:
Some have, perhaps, the name of chaste retain'd,
When nought of chastity itself remain'd;
But there is danger – few have means to blind
The keen-eyed world, and none to make it kind.

'"And one thing more – to free yourself from foes
Never a secret to your friend disclose;
Secrets with girls, like loaded guns with boys,
Are never valued till they make a noise;
To show how trusted, they their power display;
To show how worthy, they the trust betray;
Like pence in children's pockets secrets lie
In female bosoms – they must burn or fly.

'"Let not your heart be soften'd; if it be,
Let not the man his softening influence see;
For the most fond will sometimes tyrants prove,
And wound the bosom where they trace the love.
But to your fortune look, on that depend
For your life's comfort, comforts that attend
On wealth alone – wealth gone, they have their end."'

'Such were my mother's cares to mend my lot,
And such her pupil they succeeded not.

*

'Now, when she married, I from home was sent,
With grandmamma to keep perpetual Lent;
For she would take me on conditions cheap,

For what we scarcely could a parrot keep:
A trifle added to the daily fare
Would feed a maiden who must learn to spare.
  'With grandmamma I lived in perfect ease.
Consent to starve, and I was sure to please;
Full well I knew the painful shifts we made,
Expenses all to lessen or evade,
And tradesmen's flinty hearts to soften and persuade.
  'Poor grandmamma among the gentry dwelt
Of a small town, and all the honour felt;
Shrinking from all approaches to disgrace
That might be mark'd in so genteel a place;
Where every daily deed, as soon as done,
Ran through the town as fast as it could run: –
At dinners what appear'd – at cards who lost or won.
  'Our good appearance through the town was known,
Hunger and thirst were matters of our own;
And you would judge that she in scandal dealt
Who told on what we fed, or how we felt.

Delay Has Danger

Three weeks had past, and Richard rambles now
Far as the dinners of the day allow;
He rode to Farley Grange and Finley Mere,
That house so ancient, and that lake so clear:
He rode to Ripley through that river gay,
Where in the shallow streams the loaches play,
And stony fragments stay the winding stream,
And gilded pebbles at the bottom gleam,
Giving their yellow surface to the sun,
And making proud the waters as they run:
It is a lovely place, and at the side

Rises a mountain-rock in rugged pride;
And in that rock are shapes of shells, and forms
Of creatures in old worlds, of nameless worms,
Whose generations lived and died ere man,
A worm of other class, to crawl began.

There is a town call'd Silford, where his steed
Our traveller rested – He the while would feed
His mind by walking to and fro, to meet,
He knew not what adventure, in the street:
A stranger there, but yet a window-view
Gave him a face that he conceived he knew;
He saw a tall, fair, lovely lady, dress'd
As one whom taste and wealth had jointly bless'd;
He gazed, but soon a footman at the door
Thundering, alarm'd her, who was seen no more.

'This was the lady whom her lover bound
In solemn contract, and then proved unsound:
Of this affair I have a clouded view,
And should be glad to have it clear'd by you.'

So Richard spake, and instant George replied,
'I had the story from the injured side,
But when resentment and regret were gone,
And pity (shaded by contempt) came on.
Frail was the hero of my tale, but still
Was rather drawn by accident than will;
Some without meaning into guilt advance,
From want of guard, from vanity, from chance;
Man's weakness flies his more immediate pain,
A little respite from his fears to gain;
And takes the part that he would gladly fly,
If he had strength and courage to deny.

'But now my tale, and let the moral say,
When hope can sleep, there's danger in delay.
Not that for rashness, Richard, I would plead,
For unadvised alliance: No, indeed:

Think ere the contract – but, contracted, stand
No more debating, take the ready hand:
When hearts are willing, and when fears subside,
Trust not to time, but let the knot be tied;
For when a lover has no more to do,
He thinks in leisure, what shall I pursue?
And then who knows what objects come in view?
For when, assured, the man has nought to keep
His wishes warm and active, then they sleep:
Hopes die with fears; and then a man must lose
All the gay visions, and delicious views,
Once his mind's wealth! He travels at his ease,
Nor horrors now nor fairy-beauty sees;
When the kind goddess gives the wish'd assent,
No mortal business should the deed prevent;
But the blest youth should legal sanction seek
Ere yet the assenting blush has fled the cheek.

   'And – hear me, Richard, – man has reptile-pride
That often rises when his fears subside;
When, like a trader feeling rich, he now
Neglects his former smile, his humble bow,
And, conscious of his hoarded wealth, assumes
New airs, nor thinks how odious he becomes.

   'There is a wandering, wavering train of thought
That something seeks where nothing should be sought,
And will a self-delighted spirit move
To dare the danger of pernicious love.

   'First be it granted all was duly said
By the fond youth to the believing maid;
Let us suppose with many a sigh there came
The declaration of the deathless flame; –
And so her answer – "She was happy then,
Blest in herself, and did not think of men;

And with such comforts in her present state,
A wish to tempt it was to tempt her fate;
That she would not; but yet she would confess
With him she thought her hazard would be less;
Nay, more, she would esteem, she would regard express:
But to be brief – if he could wait and see
In a few years what his desires would be."' –

'Henry for years read months, then weeks, nor found
The lady thought his judgment was unsound;
"For months read weeks" she read it to his praise,
And had some thoughts of changing it to *days*.

'And here a short excursion let me make,
A lover tried, I think, for lovers' sake;
And teach the meaning in a lady's mind
When you can none in her expressions find:
Words are design'd that meaning to convey,
But often *Yea* is hidden in a *Nay!*
And what the charmer wills, some gentle hints betray.

'Then, too, when ladies mean to yield at length,
They match their reasons with the lover's strength,
And, kindly cautious, will no force employ
But such as he can baffle or destroy.

'As when heroic lovers beauty woo'd,
And were by magic's mighty art withstood,
The kind historian, for the dame afraid,
Gave to the faithful knight the stronger aid.

'A downright *No!* would make a man despair,
Or leave for kinder nymph the cruel fair;
But '*No!* because I'm very happy now,
Because I dread th' irrevocable vow,
Because I fear papa will not approve,
Because I love not – No, I cannot love;
Because you men of Cupid make a jest,
Because – in short, a single life is best.'
A *No!* when back'd by reasons of such force,

Invites approach, and will recede of course.

  'Ladies, like towns besieged, for honour's sake,
Will some defence or its appearance make;
On first approach there's much resistance made,
And conscious weakness hides in bold parade;
With lofty looks, and threat'nings stern and proud,
"Come, if you dare," is said in language loud,
But if th' attack be made with care and skill,
"Come," says the yielding party, "if you will;"
Then each the other's valiant acts approve,
And twine their laurels in a wreath of love. –

  'We now retrace our tale, and forward go, –
Thus Henry rightly read Cecilia's No!
His prudent father, who had duly weigh'd,
And well approved, the fortune of the maid,
Not much resisted, just enough to show
He knew his power, and would his son should know.

  '"Harry, I will, while I your bargain make,
That you a journey to our patron take:
I know her guardian; care will not become
A lad when courting; as you must be dumb,
You may be absent; I for you will speak,
And ask what you are not supposed to seek."

  'Then came the parting hour, and what arise
When lovers part! expressive looks and eyes,
Tender and tear-full, – many a fond adieu,
And many a call the sorrow to renew;
Sighs such as lovers only can explain,
And words that they might undertake in vain.

  'Cecilia liked it not; she had, in truth,
No mind to part with her enamour'd youth;
But thought it foolish thus themselves to cheat,
And part for nothing but again to meet.

  'Now Henry's father was a man whose heart
Took with his interest a decided part;

He knew his lordship, and was known for acts
That I omit, – they were acknowledged facts;
An interest somewhere; I the place forget,
And the good deed – no matter – 'twas a debt:
Thither must Henry, and in vain the maid
Express'd dissent – the father was obey'd.

'But though the maid was by her fears assail'd,
Her reason rose against them, and prevail'd;
Fear saw him hunting, leaping, falling – led,
Maim'd and disfigured, groaning to his bed;
Saw him in perils, duels, – dying, – dead
But Prudence answer'd, "Is not every maid
With equal cause for him she loves afraid?'
And from her guarded mind Cecilia threw
The groundless terrors that will love pursue.

'She had no doubts, and her reliance strong
Upon the honour that she would not wrong:
Firm in herself, she doubted not the truth
Of him, the chosen, the selected youth;
Trust of herself a trust in him supplied,
And she believed him faithful, though untried:
On her he might depend, in him she would confide.

'If some fond girl express'd a tender pain
Lest some fair rival should allure her swain,
To such she answer'd, with a look severe,
"Can one you doubt be worthy of your fear?"

'My lord was kind, – a month had pass'd away,
And Henry stay'd, – he sometimes named a day;
But still my lord was kind, and Henry still must stay:
His father's words to him were words of fate –
"Wait, 'tis your duty; 'tis my pleasure, wait!"
In all his walks, in hilly heath or wood,
Cecilia's form the pensive youth pursued;
In the gray morning, in the silent noon,
In the soft twilight, by the sober moon,

In those forsaken rooms, in that immense saloon;
And he, now fond of that seclusion grown,
There reads her letters, and there writes his own.
  "Here none approach," said he, "to interfere,
But I can think of my Cecilia here!"
  'But there did come – and how it came to pass
Who shall explain? – a mild and blue-eyed lass; –
It was the work of accident, no doubt –
The cause unknown – we say, "as things fall out;" –
The damsel enter'd there, in wand'ring round about:
At first she saw not Henry; and she ran,
As from a ghost, when she beheld a man.
  'She was esteem'd a beauty through the hall,
And so admitted, with consent of all;
And, like a treasure, was her beauty kept
From every guest who in the mansion slept
Whether as friends who join'd the noble pair,
Or those invited by the steward there.
  'She was the daughter of a priest, whose life
Was brief and sad: he lost a darling wife,
And Fanny then her father, who could save
But a small portion; but his all he gave,
With the fair orphan, to a sister's care,
And her good spouse: they were the ruling pair –
Steward and steward's lady – o'er a tribe,
Each under each, whom I shall not describe.
  'This grave old couple, childless and alone,
Would by their care, for Fanny's loss atone:
She had been taught in schools of honest fame;
And to the hall, as to a home, she came,
My lord assenting: yet, as meet and right,
Fanny was held from every hero's sight,
Who might in youthful error cast his eyes
On one so gentle as a lawful prize,
On border land, whom, as their right or prey,

A youth from either side might bear away.
Some handsome lover of th' inferior class
Might as a wife approve the lovely lass;
Or some invader from the class above,
Who, more presuming, would his passion prove
By asking less – love only for his love.

'This much experienced aunt her fear express'd,
And dread of old and young, of host and guest.

'"Go not, my Fanny, in their way," she cried,
"It is not right that virtue should be tried;
So, to be safe, be ever at my side."

'She was not ever at that side; but still
Observed her precepts, and obey'd her will.

'But in the morning's dawn and evening's gloom
She could not lock the damsel in her room;
And Fanny thought, "I will ascend these stairs
To see the chapel, – there are none at prayers;
None," she believed, "had yet to dress return'd,
By whom a timid girl might be discern'd."
In her slow motion, looking, as she glides,
On pictures, busts, and what she met besides,
And speaking softly to herself alone,
Or singing low in melancholy tone;
And thus she rambled through the still domain,
Room after room, again, and yet again.

'But, to retrace our story, still we say,
To this saloon the maiden took her way;
Where she beheld our youth, and frighten'd ran,
And so their friendship in her fear began.

'But dare she thither once again advance,
And still suppose the man will think it chance?
Nay, yet again, and what has chance to do
With this? – I know not: doubtless Fanny knew.

'Now, of the meeting of a modest maid
And sober youth why need we be afraid?

And when a girl's amusements are so few
As Fanny's were, what would you have her do?
Reserved herself, a decent youth to find,
And just be civil, sociable, and kind,
And look together at the setting sun,
Then at each other – What the evil done?

   'Then Fanny took my little lord to play,
And bade him not intrude on Henry's way:
"O, he intrudes not!" said the youth, and grew
Fond of the child, and would amuse him too;
Would make such faces, and assume such looks –
He loved it better than his gayest books.

   'When man with man would an acquaintance seek,
He will his thoughts in chosen language speak;
And they converse on divers themes, to find
If they possess a corresponding mind;
But man with woman has foundation laid,
And built up friendship ere a word is said:
'Tis not with words that they their wishes tell,
But with a language answering quite as well;
And thus they find, when they begin t' explore
Their way by speech, they knew it all before.

   'And now it chanced again the pair, when dark,
Met in their way, when wandering in the park;
Not in the common path, for so they might,
Without a wonder, wander day or night;
But, when in pathless ways their chance will bring
A musing pair, we do admire the thing.

   'The youth in meeting read the damsel's face,
As if he meant her inmost thoughts to trace;
On which her colour changed, as if she meant
To give her aid, and help his kind intent.

   'Both smiled and parted, but they did not speak –
The smile implied, "Do tell me what you seek:"
They took their different ways with erring feet,

And met again, surprised that they could meet;
Then must they speak – and something of the air
Is always ready – "'Tis extremely fair!"

"It was so pleasant!" Henry said; "the beam
Of that sweet light so brilliant on the stream;
And chiefly yonder, where that old cascade
Has for an age its simple music made;
All so delightful, soothing, and serene!
Do you not feel it? not enjoy the scene?
Something it has that words will not express,
But rather hide, and make th' enjoyment less·
'Tis what our souls conceive, 'tis what our hearts confess."

'Poor Fanny's heart at these same words confess'd
How well he painted, and how rightly guess'd;
And, while they stood admiring their retreat,
Henry found something like a mossy seat;
But Fanny sat not; no, she rather pray'd
That she might leave him, she was so afraid.

"Not, sir, of you; your goodness I can trust,
But folks are so censorious and unjust,
They make no difference, they pay no regard
To our true meaning, which is very hard
And very cruel; great the pain it cost
To lose such pleasure, but it must be lost:
Did people know how free from thought of ill
One's meaning is, their malice would be still."

'At this she wept; at least a glittering gem
Shone in each eye, and there was fire in them,
For as they fell, the sparkles, at his feet,
He felt emotions very warm and sweet.

"A lovely creature! not more fair than good
By all admired, by some, it seems, pursued,
Yet self-protected by her virtue's force
And conscious truth – What evil in discourse
With one so guarded, who is pleased to trust

Herself with me, reliance strong and just?"
  'Our lover then believed he must not seem
Cold to the maid who gave him her esteem;
Not manly this; Cecilia had his heart,
But it was lawful with his time to part;
It would be wrong in her to take amiss
A virtuous friendship for a girl like this;
False or disloyal he would never prove,
But kindness here took nothing from his love:
Soldiers to serve a foreign prince are known,
When not on present duty to their own;
So, though our bosom's queen we still prefer,
We are not always on our knees to her.
"Cecilia present, witness yon fair moon,
And yon bright orbs, that fate would change as soon
As my devotion; but the absent sun
Cheers us no longer when his course is run;
And then those starry twinklers may obtain
A little worship till she shines again."
  'The father still commanded "Wait awhile,"
And the son answer'd in submissive style,
Grieved, but obedient; and obedience teased
His lady's spirit more than grieving pleased:
That he should grieve in absence was most fit,
But not that he to absence should submit;
And in her letters might be traced reproof,
Distant indeed, but visible enough;
This should the wandering of his heart have stay'd;
Alas! the wanderer was the vainer made.
  'The parties daily met, as by consent,
And yet it always seem'd by accident;
Till in the nymph the shepherd had been blind
If he had fail'd to see a manner kind,
With that expressive look, that seem'd to say,
"You do not speak, and yet you see you may."

'O! yes, he saw, and he resolved to fly,
And blamed his heart, unwilling to comply:
He sometimes wonder'd how it came to pass,
That he had all this freedom with the lass;
Reserved herself, with strict attention kept,
And care and vigilance that never slept:
"How is it thus that they a beauty trust
With me, who feel the confidence is just?
And they, too, feel it; yes, they may confide."
He said in folly, and he smiled in pride.

''Tis thus our secret passions work their way,
And the poor victims know not they obey.

'Familiar now became the wandering pair,
And there was pride and joy in Fanny's air;
For though his silence did not please the maid,
She judged him only modest and afraid;
The gentle dames are ever pleased to find
Their lovers dreading they should prove unkind;
So, blind by hope, and pleased with prospects gay,
The generous beauty gave her heart away
Before he said, "I love!" – alas! he dared not say.

'Cecilia yet was mistress of his mind,
But oft he wished her, like his Fanny, kind;
Her fondness sooth'd him, for the man was vain,
And he perceived that he could give her pain:
Cecilia liked not to profess her love,
But Fanny ever was the yielding dove;
Tender and trusting, waiting for the word,
And then prepared to hail her bosom's lord.
Cecilia once her honest love avow'd,
To make him happy, not to make him proud;
But she would not, for every asking sigh,
Confess the flame that waked his vanity;
But this poor maiden, every day and hour,
Would, by fresh kindness, feed the growing power;

And he indulged, vain being! in the joy,
That he alone could raise it, or destroy;
A present good, from which he dared not fly,
Cecilia absent, and his Fanny by.

'O! vain desire of youth, that in the hour
Of strong temptation, when he feels the power,
And knows how daily his desires increase,
Yet will he wait, and sacrifice his peace,
Will trust to chance to free him from the snare,
Of which, long since, his conscience said beware!
Or look for strange deliverance from that ill,
That he might fly, could he command the will!
How can he freedom from the future seek,
Who feels already that he grows too weak?
And thus refuses to resist, till time
Removes the power, and makes the way for crime:
Yet thoughts he had, and he would think, "Forego
My dear Cecilia? not for kingdoms! No!
But may I, ought I not the friend to be
Of one who feels this fond regard for me?
I wrong no creature by a kindness lent
To one so gentle, mild and innocent;
And for that fair one, whom I still adore,
By feeling thus I think of her the more;"
And not unlikely, for our thoughts will tend
To those whom we are conscious we offend.

'Had Reason whisper'd, "Has Cecilia leave
Some gentle youth in friendship to receive,
And be to him the friend that you appear
To this soft girl? – would not some jealous fear
Proclaim your thoughts, that he approach'd too near?"

'But Henry, blinded still, presumed to write
Of one in whom Cecilia would delight;
A mild and modest girl, a gentle friend,
If, as he hoped, her kindness would descend –

But what he fear'd to lose or hoped to gain
By writing thus, he had been ask'd in vain.
  'It was his purpose, every morn he rose,
The dangerous friendship he had made to close;
It was his torment nightly, ere he slept,
To feel his prudent purpose was not kept,
  'True, he has wonder'd why the timid maid
Meets him so often, and is not afraid;
And why that female dragon, fierce and keen,
Has never in their private walks been seen;
And often he has thought, "What can their silence mean?"
  '"They can have no design, or plot, or plan, –
In fact, I know not how the thing began, –
'Tis their dependence on my credit here,
And fear not, nor, in fact, have cause to fear."
  'But did that pair, who seem'd to think that all
Unwatch'd will wander and unguarded fall,
Did they permit a youth and maid to meet
Both unreproved? were they so indiscreet?
  'This sometimes enter'd Henry's mind, and then,
"Who shall account for women or for men?"
He said, "or who their secret thoughts explore?
Why do I vex me? I will think no more."
My lord of late had said, in manner kind,
"My good friend Harry, do not think us blind!"
Letters had past, though he had nothing seen,
His careful father and my lord between;
But to what purpose was to him unknown –
It might be borough business, or their own.
. .'Fanny, it seem'd, was now no more in dread,
If one approach'd, she neither fear'd nor fled:
He mused on this, – "But wherefore her alarm?
She knows me better, and she dreads no harm."
  'Something his father wrote that gave him pain:
"I know not, son, if you should yet remain; –

Be cautious, Harry, favours to procure
We strain a point, but we must first be sure:
Love is a folly, – that, indeed, is true, –
But something still is to our honour due,
So I must leave the thing to my good lord and you."

   'But from Cecilia came remonstrance strong:
"You write too darkly, and you stay too long;
We hear reports; and, Henry, – mark me well, –
I heed not every tale that triflers tell; –
Be you no trifler; dare not to believe
That I am one whom words and vows deceive:
You know your heart, your hazard you will learn,
And this your trial – instantly return."

   '"Unjust, injurious, jealous, cruel maid!
Am I a slave, of haughty words afraid?
Can she who thus commands expect to be obey'd?
O! how unlike this dear assenting soul,
Whose heart a man might at his will control!"

   'Uneasy, anxious, fill'd with self-reproof,
He now resolved to quit his patron's roof;
And then again his vacillating mind
To stay resolved, and that her pride should find:
Debating thus, his pen the lover took
And chose the words of anger and rebuke.

   'Again, yet once again, the conscious pair
Met, and "O, speak!" was Fanny's silent prayer;
And, "I must speak," said the embarrass'd youth,
"Must save my honour, must confess the truth:
Then I must love her; but, by slow degrees,
She will regain her peace, and I my ease."

   'Ah! foolish man! to virtue true nor vice,
He buys distress, and self-esteem the price;
And what his gain? – a tender smile and sigh
From a fond girl to feed his vanity.

   'Thus every day they lived, and every time

They met, increased his anguish and his crime.
'Still in their meetings they were ofttimes nigh
The darling theme, and then past trembling by;
On those occasions Henry often tried
For the sad truth – and then his heart denied
The utterance due: thus daily he became
The prey of weakness, vanity, and shame.
'But soon a day, that was their doubts to close,
On the fond maid and thoughtless youth arose.
'Within the park, beside the bounding brook,
The social pair their usual ramble took;
And there the steward found them: they could trace
News in his looks, and gladness in his face.
'He was a man of riches, bluff and big,
With clean brown broad-cloth, and with white cut wig:
He bore a cane of price, with riband tied,
And a fat spaniel waddled at his side:
To every being whom he met he gave
His looks expressive; civil, gay, or grave,
But condescending all; and each declared
How much he govern'd, and how well he fared.
'This great man bow'd, not humbly, but his bow
Appear'd familiar converse to allow:
The trembling Fanny, as he came in view,
Within the chestnut grove in fear withdrew;
While Henry wonder'd not without a fear,
Of that which brought th' important man so near:
Doubt was dispersed by – "My esteem'd young man!"
As he with condescending grace began –
'"Though you with youthful frankness nobly trust
Your Fanny's friends, and doubtless think them just;
Though you have not, with craving soul, applied
To us, and ask'd the fortune of your bride,
Be it our care that you shall not lament
That love has made you so improvident.

'"An orphan maid – Your patience! you shall have
Your time to speak, I now attention crave; –
Fanny, dear girl! has in my spouse and me
Friends of a kind we wish our friends to be,
None of the poorest – nay, sir, no reply,
You shall not need – and we are born to die:
And one yet crawls on earth, of whom, I say,
That what he has he cannot take away;
Her mother's father, one who has a store
Of this world's good, and always looks for more;
But, next his money, loves the girl at heart,
And she will have it when they come to part."

'"Sir," said the youth, his terrors all awake,
"Hear me, I pray, I beg, – for mercy's sake!
Sir, were the secrets of my soul confess'd,
Would you admit the truths that I protest
Are such – your pardon" – "Pardon! good, my friend,
I not alone will pardon, I commend:
Think you that I have no remembrance left
Of youthful love, and Cupid's cunning theft?
How nymphs will listen when their swains persuade,
How hearts are gain'd, and how exchange is made? –
Come, sir, your hand" – "In mercy, hear me now!"
"I cannot hear you, time will not allow:
You know my station, what on me depends,
For ever needed – but we part as friends;
And here comes one who will the whole explain,
My better self – and we shall meet again."

'"Sir, I entreat" – "Then be entreaty made
To her, a woman, one you may persuade;
A little teasing, but she will comply,
And loves her niece too fondly to deny."

'"O! he is mad, and miserable I!"
Exclaim'd the youth; "But let me now collect
My scatter'd thoughts, I something must effect."

'Hurrying she came – "Now, what has he confess'd,
Ere I could come to set your heart at rest?
What! he has grieved you! Yet he, too, approves
The thing! but man will tease you, if he loves.

'"But now for business: tell me, did you think
That we should always at your meetings wink?
Think you, you walk'd unseen? There are who bring
To me all secrets – O, you wicked thing!

'"Poor Fanny! now I think I see her blush,
All red and rosy, when I beat the bush;
And hide your secret, said I, if you dare;
So out it came, like an affrighten'd hare.

'"Miss! said I gravely; and the trembling maid
Pleased me at heart to see her so afraid;
And then she wept; – now, do remember this,
Never to chide her when she does amiss;
For she is tender as the callow bird,
And cannot bear to have her temper stirr'd; –
Fanny, I said, then whisper'd her the name,
And caused such looks – Yes, yours are just the same;
But hear my story – When your love was known
For this our child – she is, in fact, our own –
Then, first debating, we agreed at last
To seek my lord, and tell him what had past."

'"To tell the earl?"

               "Yes, truly, and why not?
And then together we contrived our plot."

'"Eternal God!"

             "Nay, be not so surprised, –
In all the matter we were well advised;
We saw my lord, and Lady Jane was there,
And said to Johnson, 'Johnson, take a chair:'
True, we are servants in a certain way,
But in the higher places so are they;
We are obey'd in ours, and they in theirs obey –

So Johnson bow'd, for that was right and fit,
And had no scruple with the earl to sit –
Why look you so impatient while I tell
What they debated ? – you must like it well.

  ' " 'Let them go on,' our gracious earl began;
'They will go off,' said, joking, my good man:
'Well!' said the countess, – she's a lover's friend, –
'What if they do, they make the speedier end' –
But be you more composed, for that dear child
Is with her joy and apprehension wild:
O! we have watch'd you on from day to day,
'There go the lovers!' we were wont to say –
But why that look?' –
                     "Dear madam, I implore
A single moment!"
                   "I can give no more:
Here are your letters – that's a female pen,
Said I to Fanny – ' 'tis his sister's, then,'
Replied the maid. – No! never must you stray;
Or hide your wanderings, if you should, I pray;
I know, at least I fear, the best may err,
But keep the by-walks of your life from her:
That youth should stray is nothing to be told,
When they have sanction in the grave and old,
Who have no call to wander and transgress,
But very love of change and wantonness.

  ' "I prattle idly, while your letters wait,
And then my lord has much that he would state,
All good to you – do clear that clouded face,
And with good looks your lucky lot embrace.

  ' "Now, mind that none with her divide your heart,
For she would die ere lose the smallest part;
And I rejoice that all has gone so well,
For who th' effect of Johnson's rage can tell?
He had his fears when you began to meet,

But I assured him there was no deceit:
He is a man who kindness will requite,
But injured once, revenge is his delight,
And he would spend the best of his estates
To ruin, goods and body, them he hates;
While he is kind enough when he approves
A deed that's done, and serves the man he loves:
Come, read your letters – I must now be gone,
And think of matters that are coming on."

  'Henry was lost, – his brain confused, his soul
Dismay'd and sunk, his thoughts beyond control,
Borne on by terror, he foreboding read
Cecilia's letter! and his courage fled;
All was a gloomy, dark, and dreadful view,
He felt him guilty, but indignant too: –
And as he read, he felt the high disdain
Of injured men – "She may repent in vain."

  'Cecilia much had heard, and told him all
That scandal taught – "A servant at the hall,
Or servant's daughter, in the kitchen bred,
Whose father would not with her mother wed,
Was now his choice! a blushing fool, the toy,
Or the attempted, both of man and boy;
More than suspected, but without the wit
Or the allurements for such creatures fit;
Not virtuous though unfeeling, cold as ice
And yet not chaste, the weeping fool of vice;
Yielding, not tender; feeble, not refined;
Her form insipid, and without a mind.

  '"Rival! she spurn'd the word; but let him stay,
Warn'd as he was! beyond the present day,
Whate'er his patron might object to this,
The uncle-butler, or the weeping miss –
Let him from this one single day remain,
And then return! he would to her, in vain;

There let him then abide, to earn, or crave
Food undeserved! and be with slaves a slave."
   'Had reason guided anger, govern'd zeal,
Or chosen words to make a lover feel,
She might have saved him – anger and abuse
Will but defiance and revenge produce.
   '"Unjust and cruel, insolent and proud!"
He said, indignant, and he spoke aloud.
"Butler! and servant! Gentlest of thy sex,
Thou wouldst not thus a man who loved thee vex;
Thou wouldst not thus to vile report give ear,
Nor thus enraged for fancied crimes appear;
I know not what, dear maid! – if thy soft smiles were here."
And then, that instant, there appear'd the maid,
By his sad looks in her reproach dismay'd;
Such timid sweetness, and so wrong'd, did more
Than all her pleading tenderness before.
   'In that weak moment, when disdain and pride,
And fear and fondness, drew the man aside,
In this weak moment – "Wilt thou," he began,
"Be mine?" and joy o'er all her features ran;
"I will!" she softly whisper'd; but the roar,
Of cannon would not strike his spirit more;
Ev'n as his lips the lawless contract seal'd
He felt that conscience lost her seven-fold shield,
And honour fled; but still he spoke of love,
And all was joy in the consenting dove.
   'That evening all in fond discourse was spent,
When the sad lover to his chamber went,
To think on what had past, to grieve and to repent:
Early he rose, and look'd with many a sigh
On the red light that fill'd the eastern sky;
Oft had he stood before, alert and gay,
To hail the glories of the new-born day:
But now dejected, languid, listless, low,

He saw the wind upon the water blow,
And the cold stream curl'd onward as the gale
From the pine-hill blew harshly down the dale;
On the right side the youth a wood survey'd,
With all its dark intensity of shade;
Where the rough wind alone was heard to move,
In this, the pause of nature and of love,
When now the young are rear'd, and when the old,
Lost to the tie, grow negligent and cold –
Far to the left he saw the huts of men,
Half hid in mist, that hung upon the fen;
Before him swallows, gathering for the sea,
Took their short flights, and twitter'd on the lea;
And near the bean-sheaf stood, the harvest done,
And slowly blacken'd in the sickly sun;
All these were sad in nature, or they took
Sadness from him, the likeness of his look,
And of his mind – he ponder'd for a while,
Then met his Fanny with a borrow'd smile.

  'Not much remain'd; for money and my lord
Soon made the father of the youth accord;
His prudence half resisted, half obey'd,
And scorn kept still the guardians of the maid:
Cecilia never on the subject spoke,
She seem'd as one who from a dream awoke;
So all was peace, and soon the married pair
Fix'd with fair fortune in a mansion fair.

  'Five years had past, and what was Henry then?
The most repining of repenting men;
With a fond, teasing, anxious wife, afraid
Of all attention to another paid;
Yet powerless she her husband to amuse,
Lives but t' entreat, implore, resent, accuse;
Jealous and tender, conscious of defects,
She merits little, and yet much expects;

She looks for love that now she cannot see,
And sighs for joy that never more can be;
On his retirements her complaints intrude,
And fond reproof endears his solitude:
While he her weakness (once her kindness) sees,
And his affections in her languor freeze;
Regret, uncheck'd by hope, devours his mind,
He feels unhappy, and he grows unkind.

'"Fool! to be taken by a rosy cheek,
And eyes that cease to sparkle or to speak;
Fool! for this child my freedom to resign,
When one the glory of her sex was mine;
While from this burthen to my soul I hide,
To think what Fate has dealt, and what denied.

'"What fiend possess'd me when I tamely gave
My forced assent to be an idiot's slave?
Her beauty vanish'd, what for me remains?
Th' eternal clicking of the galling chains:
Her person truly I may think my own,
Seen without pleasure, without triumph shown:
Doleful she sits her children at her knees,
And gives up all her feeble powers to please;
Whom I, unmoved, or moved with scorn, behold,
Melting as ice, as vapid and as cold."

'Such was his fate, and he must yet endure
The self-contempt that no self-love can cure:
Some business call'd him to a wealthy town
When unprepared for more than Fortune's frown;
There at a house he gave his luckless name,
The master absent, and Cecilia came;
Unhappy man! he could not, dared not speak,
But look'd around, as if retreat to seek:
This she allow'd not; but, with brow severe,
Ask'd him his business, sternly bent to hear;
He had no courage, but he view'd that face

As if he sought for sympathy and grace;
As if some kind returning thought to trace:
In vain; not long he waited, but with air,
That of all grace compell'd him to despair,
She rang the bell, and, when a servant came,
Left the repentant traitor to his shame;
But, going, spoke, "Attend this person out,
And if he speaks, hear what he comes about!"
Then, with cool curtesy, from the room withdrew,
That seem'd to say, "Unhappy man, adieu!"
  'Thus will it be when man permits a vice
First to invade his heart, and then entice;
When wishes vain and undefined arise,
And that weak heart deceive, seduce, surprise;
When evil Fortune works on Folly's side,
And rash Resentment adds a spur to Pride;
Then life's long troubles from those actions come,
In which a moment may decide our doom.'

from Lady Barbara

  'O! tell me not of years, – can she be old?
Those eyes, those lips, can man unmoved behold?
Has time that bosom chill'd? are cheeks so rosy cold?
No, she is young, or I her love t' engage
Will grow discreet, and that will seem like age:
But speak it not; Death's equalizing arm
Levels not surer than Love's stronger charm,
That bids all inequalities be gone,
That laughs at rank, that mocks comparison.
  'There is not young or old, if Love decrees,
He levels orders, he confounds degrees;

There is not fair, or dark, or short, or tall,
Or grave, or sprightly – Love reduces all;
From each abundant good a portion takes,
And for each want a compensation makes;
Then tell me not of years – Love, power divine,
Takes, as he wills, from hers, and gives to mine.
  'And she, in truth, was lovely – Time had strown
No snows on her, though he so long had flown;
The purest damask blossom'd in her cheek,
The eyes said all that eyes are wont to speak;
Her pleasing person she with care adorn'd,
Nor arts that stay the flying graces scorn'd;
Nor held it wrong these graces to renew,
Or give the fading rose its opening hue:
Yet few there were who needed less the art
To hide an error, or a grace impart.

from The Widow

  'Harriet at school was very much the same
As other misses, and so home she came,
Like other ladies, there to live and learn,
To wait her season, and to take her turn.
  'Their husbands maids as priests their livings gain,
The best, they find, are hardest to obtain;
On those that offer both awhile debate –
"I need not take it, it is not so late;
Better will come if we will longer stay,
And strive to put ourselves in fortune's way:"
And thus they wait, till many years are past,
For what comes slowly – *but it comes at last*.
  'Harriet was wedded, – but it must be said,
The vow'd obedience was not duly paid:

Hers was an easy man, – it gave him pain
To hear a lady murmur and complain:
He was a merchant, whom his father made
Rich in the gains of a successful trade:
A lot more pleasant, or a view more fair,
Has seldom fallen to a youthful pair.

   'But what is faultless in a world like this?
In every station something seems amiss:
The lady, married, found the house too small –
"Two shabby parlours, and that ugly hall!
Had we a cottage somewhere, and could meet
One's friends and favourites in one's snug retreat;
Or only join a single room to these,
It would be living something at our ease,
And have one's self, at home, the comfort that one sees."

   'Such powers of reason, and of mind such strength,
Fought with man's fear, and they prevail'd at length:
The room was built, – and Harriet did not know
A prettier dwelling, either high or low;
But Harriet loved such conquests, loved to plead
With her reluctant man, and to succeed;
It was such pleasure to prevail o'er one
Who would oppose the thing that still was done,
Who never gain'd the race, but yet would groan and run.

   'But there were times when love and pity gave
Whatever thoughtless vanity could crave:
She now the carriage chose with freshest name,
And was in quite a fever till it came;
But can a carriage be alone enjoy'd?
The pleasure not partaken is destroy'd;
"I must have some good creature to attend
On morning visits as a kind of friend."

   'A courteous maiden then was found to sit
Beside the lady, for her purpose fit,
Who had been train'd in all the soothing ways

And servile duties from her early days;
One who had never from her childhood known
A wish fulfill'd, a purpose of her own:
Her part it was to sit beside the dame,
And give relief in every want that came;
To soothe the pride, to watch the varying look,
And bow in silence to the dumb rebuke.
  'This supple being strove with all her skill
To draw her master's to her lady's will;
For they were like the magnet and the steel,
At times so distant that they could not feel;
Then would she gently move them, till she saw
That to each other they began to draw;
And then would leave them, sure on her return
In Harriet's joy her conquest to discern.
  'She was a mother now, and grieved to find
The nursery window caught the eastern wind;
What could she do with fears like these oppress'd?
She built a room all window'd to the west;
For sure in one so dull, so bleak, so old,
She and her children must expire with cold:
Meantime the husband murmur'd – "So he might;
She would be judged by Cousins – Was it right?"
  'Water was near them, and her mind afloat,
The lady saw a cottage and a boat,
And thought what sweet excursions they might make,
How they might sail, what neighbours they might take,
And nicely would she deck the lodge upon the lake.
  'She now prevail'd by habit; had her will,
And found her patient husband sad and still:
Yet this displeased; she gain'd, indeed, the prize,
But not the pleasure of her victories;
Was she a child to be indulged? He knew
She would have right, but would have reason too.

from William Bailey

'Frances, like William, felt her heart incline
To neat attire – but Frances would be fine:
Though small the farm, the farmer's daughter knew
Her rank in life, and she would have it too:
This, and this only, gave the lover pain,
He thought it needless and he judged it vain:
Advice in hints he to the fault applied,
And talk'd of sin, of vanity, and pride.

'"And what is proud," said Frances, "but to stand
Singing at church, and sawing thus your hand?
Looking at heaven above, as if to bring
The holy angels down to hear you sing?
And when you write, you try with all your skill,
And cry, no wonder that you wrote so ill!
For you were ever to yourself a rule,
And humbly add, you never were at school –
Is that not proud? – And I have heard beside,
The proudest creatures have the humblest pride:
If you had read the volumes I have hired,
You'd see your fault, nor try to be admired;
For they who read such books can always tell
The fault within, and read the mind as well."

'William had heard of hiring books before,
He knew she read, and he inquired no more;
On him the subject was completely lost,
What he regarded was the time and cost;
Yet that was trifling – just a present whim,
"Novels and stories! what were they to him?"

'With such slight quarrels, or with those as slight,
They lived in love, and dream'd of its delight.
Her duties Fanny knew, both great and small,
And she with diligence observed them all;

If e'er she fail'd a duty to fulfil,
'Twas childish error, not rebellious will;
For her much reading, though it touch'd her heart,
Could neither vice nor indolence impart.
　'Yet, when from William and her friends retired,
She found her reading had her mind inspired
With hopes and thoughts of high mysterious things,
Such as the early dream of kindness brings;
And then she wept, and wonder'd as she read,
And new emotions in her heart were bred:
She sometimes fancied that when love was true
'Twas more than she and William ever knew;
More than the shady lane in summer-eve,
More than the sighing when he took his leave;
More than his preference when the lads advance
And choose their partners for the evening dance;
Nay, more than midnight thoughts and morning dreams,
Or talk when love and marriage are the themes;
In fact, a something not to be defined,
Of all subduing, all commanding kind,
That fills the fondest heart, that rules the proudest mind.

from The Cathedral-Walk

　'In an autumnal evening, cool and still,
The sun just dropp'd beneath a distant hill,
The children gazing on the quiet scene,
Then rose in glory Night's majestic queen;
And pleasant was the chequer'd light and shade
Her golden beams and maple shadows made;
An ancient tree that in the garden grew,
And that fair picture on the gravel threw.
　'Then all was silent, save the sounds that make

Silence more awful, while they faintly break;
The frighten'd bat's low shriek, the beetle's hum,
With nameless sounds we know not whence they come.
   'Such was the evening; and that ancient seat
The scene were then some neighbours chanced to meet;
Up to the door led broken steps of stone,
Whose dewy surface in the moonlight shone;
On vegetation, that with progress slow
Where man forbears to fix his foot, will grow;
The window's depth and dust repell'd the ray
Of the moon's light and of the setting day;
Pictures there were, and each display'd a face
And form that gave their sadness to the place;
The frame and canvas show'd that worms unseen,
Save in their works, for years had working been;
A fire of brushwood on the irons laid
All the dull room in fitful views display'd,
And with its own wild light in fearful forms array'd.
   'In this old Hall, in this departing day,
Assembled friends and neighbours, grave and gay,
When one good lady at a picture threw
A glance that caused inquiry – "Tell us who?"
   '"That was a famous warrior; one, they said,
That by a spirit was awhile obey'd;
In all his dreadful battles he would say,
'Or win or lose, I shall escape to-day;'
And though the shot as thick as hail came round,
On no occasion he received a wound;
He stood in safety, free from all alarm,
Protected, heaven forgive him, by his charm:
But he forgot the date, till came the hour
When he no more had the protecting power;
And then he bade his friends around farewell!
'I fall!' he cried, and in the instant fell.
   '"Behold those infants in the frame beneath!

A witch offended wrought their early death;
She form'd an image, made as wax to melt,
And each the wasting of the figure felt;
The hag confess'd it when she came to die,
And no one living can the truth deny.
　'"But see a beauty in King William's days,
With that long waist, and those enormous stays;
She had three lovers, and no creature knew
The one preferr'd, or the discarded two;
None could the secret of her bosom see;
Loving, poor maid, th' attention of the three,
She kept such equal weight in either scale,
'Twas hard to say who would at last prevail;
Thus you may think in either heart arose
A jealous anger, and the men were foes;
Each with himself concluded, two aside,
The third may make the lovely maid his bride:
This caused their fate – It was on Thursday night,
The deed was done, and bloody was the fight;
Just as she went, poor thoughtless girl! to prayers,
Ran wild the maid with horror up the stairs;
Pale as a ghost, but not a word she said,
And then the lady utter'd, 'Coates is dead!'
　'"Then the poor damsel found her voice and cried,
'Ran through the body, and that instant died!
But he pronounced your name, and so was satisfied.'
A second fell, and he who did survive
Was kept by skill and sovereign drugs alive;
'O! would she see me!' he was heard to say,
'No! I'll torment him to his dying day!'
The maid exclaim'd, and every Thursday night
Her spirit came his wretched soul to fright;
Once as she came he cried aloud 'Forgive!'
'Never!' she answer'd, 'never while you live,
Nor when you die, as long as time endures;

You have my torment been, and I'll be yours!'
That is the lady, and the man confess'd
Her vengeful spirit would not let him rest."

from Smugglers and Poachers

  "'Twas past the dead of night, when every sound
That nature mingles might be heard around;
But none from man, — man's feeble voice was hush'd,
Where rivers swelling roar'd, and woods were crush'd;
Hurried by these, the wife could sit no more,
But must the terrors of the night explore.
  'Softly she left her door, her garden gate,
And seem'd as then committed to her fate;
To every horrid thought and doubt a prey,
She hurried on, already lost her way;
Oft as she glided on in that sad night,
She stopp'd to listen, and she look'd for light;
An hour she wander'd, and was still to learn
Aught of her husband's safety or return:
A sudden break of heavy clouds could show
A place she knew not, but she strove to know;
Still further on she crept with trembling feet,
With hope a friend, with fear a foe to meet:
And there was something fearful in the sight,
And in the sound of what appear'd to-night;
For now, of night and nervous terror bred,
Arose a strong and superstitious dread;
She heard strange noises, and the shapes she saw
Of fancied beings bound her soul in awe.
  'The moon was risen, and she sometimes shone
Through thick white clouds, that flew tumultuous on,
Passing beneath her with an eagle's speed,

That her soft light imprison'd and then freed;
The fitful glimmering through the hedge-row green
Gave a strange beauty to the changing scene;
And roaring winds and rushing waters lent
Their mingled voice that to the spirit went.

  'To these she listen'd; but new sounds were heard,
And sight more startling to her soul appear'd;
There were low lengthen'd tones with sobs between,
And near at hand, but nothing yet was seen;
She hurried on, and "Who is there?" she cried,
"A dying wretch!" – was from the earth replied.

  'It was her lover, was the man she gave,
The price she paid, himself from death to save;
With whom, expiring, she must kneel and pray,
While the soul flitted from the shivering clay
That press'd the dewy ground, and bled its life away!

  'This was the part that duty bade her take,
Instant and ere her feelings were awake;
But now they waked to anguish; there came then,
Hurrying with lights, loud-speaking, eager men.

Posthumous Tales

from The Family of Love

Men who by labours live, and, day by day,
Work, weave, and spin their active lives away:
Like bees industrious, they for others strive,
With, now and then, some murmuring in the hive.

　　James was a churchman – 'twas his pride and boast;
Loyal his heart, and 'Church and King' his toast;
He for Religion might not warmly feel,
But for the Church he had abounding zeal.

　　Yet no dissenting sect would he condemn,
'They're nought to us,' said he, 'nor we to them;
'Tis innovation of our own I hate,
Whims and inventions of a modern date.

　　'Why send you Bibles all the world about,
That men may read amiss, and learn to doubt?
Why teach the children of the poor to read,
That a new race of doubters may succeed?
Now can you scarcely rule the stubborn crew,
And what if they should know as much as you?
Will a man labour when to learning bred,
Or use his hands who can employ his head?
Will he a clerk or master's self obey,
Who thinks himself as well-inform'd as they?'

　　These were his favourite subjects – these he chose,
And where he ruled no creature durst oppose.

　　'We are rich,' quoth James; 'but if we thus proceed,
And give to all, we shall be poor indeed:
In war we subsidise the world – in peace
We christianise – our bounties never cease:
We learn each stranger's tongue, that they with ease
May read translated Scriptures, if they please;

We buy them presses, print them books, and then
Pay and export poor, learned, pious men;
Vainly we strive a fortune now to get,
So tax'd by private claims, and public debt,'
    Still he proceeds – 'You make your prisons light,
Airy and clean, your robbers to invite;
And in such ways your pity show to vice,
That you the rogues encourage, and entice.'
    For lenient measures James had no regard –
'Hardship,' he said, 'must work upon the hard;
Labour and chains such desperate men require;
To soften iron you must use the fire.'
    Active himself, he labour'd to express,
In his strong words, his scorn of idleness;
From him in vain the beggar sought relief –
'Who will not labour is an idle thief,
Stealing from those who will;' he knew not how
For the untaught and ill-taught to allow,
Children of want and vice, inured to ill,
Unchain'd the passions, and uncurb'd the will.
    Alas! he look'd but to his own affairs,
Or to the rivals in his trade, and theirs:
Knew not the thousands who must all be fed,
Yet ne'er were taught to earn their daily bread;
Whom crimes, misfortunes, errors only teach
To seek their food where'er within their reach,
Who for their parents' sins, or for their own,
Are now as vagrants, wanderers, beggars known,
Hunted and hunting through the world, to share
Alms and contempt, and shame and scorn to bear;
Whom Law condemns, and Justice, with a sigh,
Pursuing, shakes her sword and passes by. –
If to the prison we should these commit,
They for the gallows will be render'd fit.

*

Rigid she was, persisting in her grief,
Fond of complaint, and adverse to relief.
In her religion she was all severe,
And as she was, was anxious to appear.
When sorrow died restraint usurp'd the place,
And sate in solemn state upon her face,
Reading she loved not, nor would deign to waste
Her precious time on trifling works of taste;
Though what she did with all that precious time
We know not, but to waste it was a crime –
As oft she said, when with a serious friend
She spent the hours as duty bids us spend;
To read a novel was a kind of sin –
Albeit once Clarissa took her in;
And now of late she heard with much surprise,
Novels there were that made a compromise
Betwixt amusement and religion; these
Might charm the worldly, whom the stories please,
And please the serious, whom the sense would charm,
And thus indulging, be secured from harm –
A happy thought, when from the foe we take
His arms, and use them for religion's sake.

Her Bible she perused by day, by night;
It was her task – she said 'twas her delight;
Found in her room, her chamber, and her pew,
For ever studied, yet for ever new –
All must be new that we cannot retain,
And new we find it when we read again.

The hardest texts she could with ease expound,
And meaning for the most mysterious found,
Knew which of dubious senses to prefer:
The want of Greek was not a want in her; –
Instinctive light no aid from Hebrew needs –
But full conviction without study breeds;
O'er mortal powers by inborn strength prevails,
Where Reason trembles, and where Learning fails.

from The Equal Marriage

There are gay nymphs whom serious matrons blame,
And men adventurous treat as lawful game, –
Misses who strive, with deep and practised arts,
To gain and torture inexperienced hearts;
The hearts entangled they in pride retain,
And at their pleasure make them feel their chain:
For this they learn to manage air and face,
To look a virtue, and to act a grace,
To be whatever men with warmth pursue –
Chaste, gay, retiring, tender, timid, true,
To-day approaching near, to-morrow just in view.
  Maria Glossip was a thing like this –
A much observing, much experienced Miss;
Who on a stranger-youth would first decide
Th' important question – 'Shall I be his bride?'
But if unworthy of a lot so bless'd,
Twas something yet to rob the man of rest;
The heart, when stricken, she with hope could feed,
Could court pursuit, and, when pursued, recede.
Hearts she had won, and with delusion fed,
With doubt bewilder'd, and with hope misled;
Mothers and rivals she had made afraid,
And wrung the breast of many a jealous maid;
Friendship, the snare of lovers, she profess'd,
And turn'd the heart's best feelings to a jest.
  Yet seem'd the Nymph as gentle as a dove,
Like one all guiltless of the game of love, –
Whose guileless innocence might well be gay;
Who had no selfish secrets to betray;
Sure, if she play'd, she knew not how to play.
Oh! she had looks so placid and demure,
Not Eve, ere fallen, seem'd more meek or pure;

And yet the Tempter of the falling Eve
Could not with deeper subtilty deceive.
   A Sailor's heart the lady's kindness moved,
And winning looks, to say how well he loved;
Then left her hopeful for the stormy main,
Assured of love when he return'd again.
Alas! the gay Lieutenant reach'd the shore,
To be rejected, and was gay no more;
Wine and strong drink the bosom's pain suppress'd,
Till Death procured, what Love denied him – rest.

*

   As in some pleasant eve we view the scene,
Though cool yet calm, if joyless yet serene, –
Who has not felt a quiet still delight
In the clear, silent, love-befriending night?
The moon so sweetly bright, so softly fair,
That all but happy lovers would be there, –
Thinking there must be in her still domain
Something that soothes the sting of mortal pain;
While earth itself is dress'd in light so clear,
That they might rest contented to be here!
   Such is the night; but when the morn awakes,
The storm arises, and the forest shakes;
This mighty change the grieving travellers find,
The freezing snows fast drifting in the wind;
Firs deeply laden shake the snowy top,
Streams slowly freezing, fretting till they stop;
And void of stars the angry clouds look down
On the cold earth, exchanging frown with frown.
   Such seem'd, at first, the cottage of our pair –
Fix'd in their fondness, in their prospects fair;
Youth, health, affection, all that life supplies,
Bright as the stars that gild the cloudless skies,
Were theirs – or seem'd to be, but soon the scene
Was black as if its light had never been.

Weary full soon, and restless then they grew,
Then off the painful mask of prudence threw,
For Time has told them all; and taught them what to rue.
They long again to tread the former round
Of dissipation – 'Why should he be bound,
While his sweet inmate of the cottage sighs
For adulation, rout, and rhapsodies?
Not Love himself, did love exist, could lead
A heart like hers, that flutter'd to be freed.'

from The Farewell and Return

The whistling Boy that holds the plough,
    Lured by the tale that soldiers tell,
Resolves to part, yet knows not how
    To leave the land he loves so well.
He now rejects the thought, and now
    Looks o'er the lea, and sighs 'Farewell!'

Farewell! the pensive Maiden cries,
    Who dreams of London, dreams awake –
But when her favourite Lad she spies,
    With whom she loved her way to take,
Then Doubts within her soul arise,
    And equal Hopes her bosom shake!

Thus, like the Boy, and like the Maid,
    I wish to go, yet tarry here,
And now resolved, and now afraid:
    To minds disturb'd old views appear
In melancholy charms array'd,
    And once indifferent, now are dear.
How shall I go, my fate to learn –
And, oh! how taught shall I return?

Parham Revisited
[1814]

Yes, I behold again the place,
   The seat of joy, the source of pain;
It brings in view the form and face
   That I must never see again.

The night-bird's song that sweetly floats
   On this soft gloom – this balmy air,
Brings to the mind her sweeter notes
   That I again must never hear.

Lo! yonder shines that window's light,
   My guide, my token, heretofore;
And now again it shines as bright,
   When those dear eyes can shine no more.

Then hurry from this place away!
   It gives not now the bliss it gave;
For Death has made its charm his prey,
   And joy is buried in her grave.

Infancy – A Fragment

Who on the new-born light can back return,
And the first efforts of the soul discern –
Waked by some sweet maternal smile, no more
To sleep so long or fondly as before?
No! Memory cannot reach, with all her power,
To that new birth, that life-awakening hour.
No! all the traces of her first employ
Are keen perceptions of the senses' joy,
And their distaste – what then could they impart?
That figs were luscious, and that rods had smart.
  But, though the Memory in that dubious way
Recalls the dawn and twilight of her day,
And thus encounters, in the doubtful view,
With imperfection and distortion too;
Can she not tell us, as she looks around,
Of good and evil, which the most abound?
  Alas! and what is earthly good? 'tis lent
Evil to hide, to soften, to prevent,
By scenes and shows that cheat the wandering eye,
While the more pompous misery passes by;
Shifts and amusements that awhile succeed,
And heads are turn'd, that bosoms may not bleed:
For what is Pleasure, that we toil to gain?
'Tis but the slow or rapid flight of Pain.
Set Pleasure by, and there would yet remain,
For every nerve and sense the sting of Pain:
Set Pain aside, and fear no more the sting,
And whence your hopes and pleasures can ye bring?
No! there is not a joy beneath the skies,
That from no grief nor trouble shall arise.

Why does the Lover with such rapture fly
To his dear mistress? – He shall show us why: –
Because her absence is such cause of grief
That her sweet smile alone can yield relief.
Why, then, that smile is Pleasure: – True, yet still
'Tis but the absence of the former ill:
For, married, soon at will he comes and goes;
Then pleasures die, and pains become repose,
And he has none of these, and therefore none of those.
    Yes! looking back as early as I can,
I see the griefs that seize their subject Man,
That in the weeping Child their early reign began:
Yes! though Pain softens, and is absent since,
He still controls me like my lawful prince.
Joys I remember, like phosphoric light
Or squibs and crackers on a gala night.
Joys are like oil; if thrown upon the tide
Of flowing life, they mix not, nor subside:
Griefs are like waters on the river thrown,
They mix entirely, and become its own.
Of all the good that grew of early date,
I can but parts and incidents relate:
A guest arriving, or a borrow'd day
From school, or schoolboy triumph at some play:
And these from Pain may be deduced; for these
Removed some ill, and hence their power to please.
    But it was Misery stung me in the day
Death of an infant sister made a prey;
For then first met and moved my early fears,
A father's terrors, and a mother's tears.
Though greater anguish I have since endured, –
Some heal'd in part, some never to be cured;
Yet was there something in that first-born ill,
So new, so strange, that memory feels it still!
    That my first grief: but, oh! in after-years

Were other deaths, that call'd for other tears.
No! that I cannot, that I dare not, paint –
That patient sufferer, that enduring saint,
Holy and lovely – but all words are faint.
But here I dwell not – let me, while I can,
Go to the Child, and lose the suffering Man.

Sweet was the morning's breath, the inland tide,
And our boat gliding, where alone could glide
Small craft – and they oft touch'd on either side.
It was my first-born joy. I heard them say,
'Let the child go; he will enjoy the day.'
For children ever feel delighted when
They take their portion, and enjoy with men.
Give him the pastime that the old partake,
And he will quickly top and taw forsake.

The linnet chirp'd upon the furze as well,
To my young sense, as sings the nightingale.
Without was paradise – because within
Was a keen relish, without taint of sin.

A town appear'd – and where an infant went,
Could they determine, on themselves intent?
I lost my way, and my companions me,
And all, their comforts and tranquillity.
Mid-day it was, and, as the sun declined,
The good, found early, I no more could find:
The men drank much, to whet the appetite;
And, growing heavy, drank to make them light;
Then drank to relish joy, then further to excite.
Their cheerfulness did but a moment last;
Something fell short, or something overpast.
The lads play'd idly with the helm and oar,
And nervous women would be set on shore,
Till 'civil dudgeon' grew, and peace would smile no more.

Now on the colder water faintly shone
The sloping light – the cheerful day was gone;

Frown'd every cloud, and from the gather'd frown
The thunder burst, and rain came pattering down.
My torpid senses now my fears obey'd,
When the fierce lightning on the eye-balls play'd.
Now, all the freshness of the morning fled,
My spirits burden'd, and my heart was dead;
The female servants show'd a child their fear,
And men, full wearied, wanted strength to cheer;
And when, at length, the dreaded storm went past,
And there was peace and quietness at last,
'Twas not the morning's quiet – it was not
Pleasure revived, but Misery forgot:
It was not Joy that now commenced her reign,
But mere relief from wretchedness and Pain.

So many a day, in life's advance, I knew;
So they commenced, and so they ended too.
All Promises they – all Joy as they began!
But Joy grew less, and vanish'd as they ran!
Errors and evils came in many a form, –
The mind's delusion, and the passions' storm.

The promised joy, that like this morning rose,
Broke on my view, then clouded at its close;
E'en Love himself, that promiser of bliss,
Made his best days of pleasure end like this:
He mix'd his bitters in the cup of joy,
Nor gave a bliss uninjured by alloy.

POET TO POET

In the introductions to their personal selections from the work of poets they have admired, the individual editors write as follows:

Henryson Selected by Hugh MacDiarmid

'There is now a consensus of judgement that regards Henryson as the greatest of our great makars. Literary historians and other commentators in the bad period of the century preceding the twenties of our own century were wont to group together as the great five: Henryson, Dunbar, Douglas, Lyndsay, and King James I; but in the critical atmosphere prevailing today it is clear that Henryson (who was, with the exception of King James, the youngest of them) is the greatest.'

Herbert Selected by W. H. Auden

'The two English poets, neither of them, perhaps, major poets, whom I would most like to have known well, are William Barnes and George Herbert.

'Even if Isaac Walton had never written his life, I think that any reader of his poetry will conclude that George Herbert must have been an exceptionally good man, and exceptionally nice as well.'

Tennyson Selected by Kingsley Amis

'England notoriously had its doubts as well as its certainties, its neuroses as well as its moral health, its fits of gloom and frustration and panic as well as its complacency. Tennyson is the voice of those doubts and their accompaniments, and his genius enabled him to communicate them in such a way that we can understand them and feel them as our own. In short we know from experience just what he means. Eliot called him the saddest of all English poets, and I cannot improve on that judgement.'